A Judgement in Stone

P. Versteeg

Nijmegen,

18 · 5 · 2020

Blackbirds

2002 Nr. 3

Blackbirds, reeks voor scholieren, is een uitgave van
Wolters-Noordhoff, Groningen.

Titeloverzicht Blackbirds 2002 (ISBN 9001 55491 1)

2002/1 - Paul Theroux *The Mosquito Coast*
  (ISBN 9001 55492 X)
2002/2 - Sue Townsend *Rebuilding Coventry*
  (ISBN 9001 55493 8)
2002/3 - Ruth Rendell *A Judgement in Stone*
  (ISBN 9001 55494 6)

Ruth Rendell

A Judgement in Stone

2002
Wolters-Noordhoff, Groningen

ISBN 9001 55494 6

For Gerald Austin, with love

Chapter 1

Eunice Parchman killed the Coverdale family because she could not read or write.

There was no real motive and no premeditation; no money was gained and no security. As a result of her crime, Eunice Parchman's disability was made known not to a mere family or a handful of villagers but to the whole country. She accomplished nothing by it but disaster for herself, and all along, somewhere in her strange mind, she knew she would accomplish nothing. And yet, although her companion and partner was mad, Eunice was not. She had the awful practical sanity of the atavistic ape disguised as twentieth-century woman.

Literacy is one of the cornerstones of civilization. To be illiterate is to be deformed. And the derision that was once directed at the physical freak may, perhaps more justly, descend upon the illiterate. If he or she can live a cautious life among the uneducated all may be well, for in the country of the purblind the eyeless is not rejected. It was unfortunate for Eunice Parchman, and for them, that the people who employed her and in whose home she lived for nine months were peculiarly literate. Had they been a family of philistines, they might be alive today and Eunice free in her mysterious dark freedom of sensation and instinct and blank absence of the printed word.

*

The family belonged to the upper middle class, and they lived a

7

conventional upper-middle-class life in a country house. George Coverdale had a degree in philosophy, but since the age of thirty he had been managing director of his late father's company, Tin Box Coverdale, at Stantwich in Suffolk. With his wife and his three children, Peter, Paula and Melinda, he had occupied a large 1930-ish house on the outskirts of Stantwich until his wife died of cancer when Melinda was twelve.

Two years later, at the wedding of Paula to Brian Caswall, George met thirty-seven-year-old Jacqueline Mont. She also had been married before but had divorced her husband for desertion, and had been left with one son. George and Jacqueline fell in love more or less at first sight and were married three months later. George bought a manor house ten miles from Stantwich and went to live there with his bride, with Melinda and with Giles Mont, Peter Coverdale having at that time been married for three years.

When Eunice Parchman was engaged as their housekeeper George was fifty-seven and Jacqueline forty-two. They took an active part in the social life of the neighbourhood, and in an unobtrusive way had slipped into playing the parts of the squire and his lady. Their marriage was idyllic and Jacqueline was popular with her stepchildren, Peter, a lecturer in political economy at a northern university, Paula, now herself a mother and living in London, and Melinda, who, at twenty, was reading English at the University of Norfolk in Galwich. Her own son, Giles, aged seventeen, was still at school.

Four members of this family, George, Jacqueline and Melinda Coverdale and Giles Mont, died in the space of fifteen minutes on 14 February, St Valentine's Day. Eunice Parchman and the prosaically named Joan Smith shot them down on a Sunday evening while they were watching opera on television. Two weeks later Eunice was arrested for the crime – because she could not read.

But there was more to it than that.

Chapter 2

The gardens of Lowfield Hall are overgrown now and weeds push their way up through the gravel of the drive. One of the drawing-room windows, broken by a village boy, has been boarded up, and wisteria, killed by summer drought, hangs above the front door like an old dried net. Bare ruined choirs where late the sweet birds sang.

It has become a bleak house, fit nesting place for the birds that Dickens named Hope, Joy, Youth, Peace, Rest, Life, Dust, Ashes, Waste, Want, Ruin, Despair, Madness, Death, Cunning, Folly, Words, Wigs, Rags, Sheepskin, Plunder, Precedent, Jargon, Gammon and Spinach.

Before Eunice came, and left desolation behind her, Lowfield Hall was not like this. It was as well kept as its distant neighbours, as comfortable, as warm, as elegant, and, seemingly, as much a sanctuary as they. Its inhabitants were safe and happy, and destined surely to lead long secure lives.

But on an April day they invited Eunice in.

A little blustery wind was blowing the daffodils in the orchard, waves on a golden sea. The clouds parted and closed again, so that at one moment it was winter in the garden and at the next an uneasy summer. And in those sombre intervals it might have been snow, not the blossom of the blackthorn, that whitened the hedge.

Winter stopped at the windows. The sun brought in flashes of summer to match the pleasant warmth, and it was warm enough for Jacqueline Coverdale to sit down to breakfast in a short-sleeved dress.

She was holding a letter in her left hand on which she wore her platinum wedding ring and the diamond cluster George had given her on their engagement.

'I'm not looking forward to this at all,' she said.

'More coffee, please, darling,' said George. He loved watching her do things for him, as long as she didn't have to do too much. He loved just looking at her, so pretty, his Jacqueline, fair, slender, a Lizzie Siddal matured. Six years of marriage, and he hadn't got used to the wonder of it, the miracle that he had found her. 'Sorry,' he said. 'You're not looking forward to it? Well, we didn't get any other replies. Women aren't exactly queueing up to work for us.'

She shook her head, a quick pretty gesture. Her hair was very blonde, short and sleek. 'We could try again. I know you'll say I'm silly, George, but I had a sort of absurd hope that we'd get – well, someone like ourselves. At any rate, a reasonably educated person who was willing to take on domestic service for the sake of a nice home.'

'A "lady", as they used to say.'

Jacqueline smiled in rather a shamefaced way. 'Eva Baalham would write a better letter than this one. E. Parchman! What a way for a woman to sign her name!'

'It was correct usage for the Victorians.'

'Maybe, but we're not Victorians. Oh dear, I wish we were. Imagine a smart parlourmaid waiting on us now, and a cook busy in the kitchen.' And Giles, she thought but didn't say aloud, obliged to be well mannered and not to read at table. Had he heard any of this? Wasn't he the least bit interested? 'No income tax,' she said aloud, 'and no horrible new houses all over the countryside.'

'And no electricity either,' said George, touching the radiator behind him, 'or constant hot water, and perhaps Paula dying in childbirth.'

'I know.' Jacqueline returned to her original tack. 'But that letter, darling, and her bleak manner when she phoned. I just know she's going to be a vulgar lumpish creature who'll break the china and sweep the dust under the mats.'

'You can't know that, and it's hardly fair judging her by one letter. You want a housekeeper, not a secretary. Go and see her. You've fixed this interview, Paula's expecting you, and you'll only regret it if you let the chance go by. If she makes a bad impression on you, just tell her no, and then we'll think about trying again.'

The grandfather clock in the hall struck the first quarter after eight. George got up. 'Come along now, Giles, I believe that clock's a few minutes slow.' He kissed his wife. Very slowly Giles closed his copy of the *Baghavad Gita* which had been propped against the marmalade pot, and with a kind of concentrated lethargy extended himself to his full, emaciated, bony height. Muttering under his breath something that might have been Greek or, for all she knew, Sanscrit, he let his mother kiss his spotty cheek.

'Give my love to Paula,' said George, and off they went in the white Mercedes, George to Tin Box Coverdale, Giles to the Magnus Wythen Foundation School. Silence settled upon them in the car after George, who tried, who was determined to keep on trying, had remarked that it was a very windy day. Giles said 'Mmm'. As always, he resumed his reading. George thought, Please let this woman be all right, because I can't let Jackie keep on trying to run that enormous place, it's not fair. We shall have to move into a bungalow or something, and I don't want that, God forbid, so please let this E. Parchman be all right.

There are six bedrooms in Lowfield Hall, a drawing room, a dining room, a morning room, three bathrooms, a kitchen, and what are known as usual offices. In this case, the usual offices were the back kitchen and the gun room. On that April morning the house wasn't exactly dirty, but it wasn't clean either. There was a bluish film on all the thirty-three windows, and the film was decorated with fingerprints and finger smears: Eva Baalham's, and probably, even after two months, those of the last and most lamentable of all the au pairs. Jacqueline had worked it out once, and estimated that six thousand square feet of carpet covered the floors. This, however, was fairly clean. Old Eva loved plying the vacuum cleaner while chatting about her relations. She used a duster too, up to eye level. It was just unfortunate that her eyes happened to be about four feet nine from the ground.

Jacqueline put the breakfast things in the dishwasher, the milk and butter in the fridge. The fridge hadn't been defrosted for six weeks. Had the oven *ever* been cleaned? She went upstairs. It was awful, she ought to be ashamed of herself, she knew that, but her hand came away grey with dust from the banisters. The little bathroom, the one they called the children's bathroom, was in a hideous mess, Giles's latest acne remedy, a kind of green paste, caked all over the basin. She hadn't made the beds. Hastily she pulled the pink sheet, the blankets, the silk counterpane up over the six-foot-wide mattress she shared with George. Giles's bed could stay the way it was. She doubted if he would notice anyway – wouldn't notice if the sheets all turned purple and there was a warming pan in it instead of an electric blanket.

Attention to her own appearance she didn't skimp. She often thought it was a pity she wasn't as house-proud as she was Jacqueline-proud, but that was the way it was, that was the way *she* was. Bath, hair, hands, nails, warmer dress, sheer tights, the new dark green shoes, face painted to look *au naturel*. She put on the mink George had given her for Christmas. Now down to the orchard to pick an armful of daffodils for Paula. At any rate, she kept the garden nice, not a weed to be seen, and there wouldn't be, even in the height of summer.

Waves on a golden sea. Snowdrops nestling under the

whiter hedge. Twice already, this dry spring, she had mown the lawns, and they were plushy green. An open-air lady I am, thought Jacqueline, the wind on her face, the thin sharp scents of spring flowers delighting her. I could stand here for hours, looking at the river, the poplars in the water meadows, the Greeving Hills with all these cloud shadows racing, racing... But she had to see this woman, this E. Parchman. Time to go. If only she turns out to like housework as much as I like gardening.

She went back into the house. Was it her imagination, or did the kitchen really not smell at all nice? Out through the gun room, which was in its usual mess, lock the door, leave Lowfield Hall to accumulate more dust, grow that much more frowsty.

Jacqueline put the daffodils on the back seat of the Ford and set off to drive the seventy miles to London.

George Coverdale was an exceptionally handsome man, classic-featured, as trim of figure as when he had rowed for his university in 1939. Of his three children only one had inherited his looks, and Paula Caswall was not that one. A sweet expression and gentle eyes saved her from plainness, but pregnancy was not becoming to her, and she was in the eighth month of her second pregnancy. She had a vigorous mischievous little boy to look after, a fairly big house in Kensington to run, she was huge and tired and her ankles were swollen. Also she was frightened. Patrick's birth had been a painful nightmare, and she looked forward to this coming delivery with dread. She would have preferred to see no one and have no one see her. But she realized that her house was the obvious venue for an interview with this London-based prospective housekeeper, and being endowed with the gracious manners of the Coverdales, she welcomed her stepmother affectionately, enthused over the daffodils and complimented Jacqueline on her dress. They had lunch, and Paula listened with sympathy to Jacqueline's doubts and forbodings about what would ensue at two o'clock.

However, she was determined to take no part in this interview. Patrick had gone for his afternoon sleep, and when the doorbell rang at two minutes to two Paula did no more than show the woman in the navy blue raincoat into the living room. She left her to Jacqueline and went upstairs to lie down. But in those few seconds she spent with Eunice Parchman she felt a violent antipathy to her. Eunice affected her in that moment as she so often affected others. It was as if a coldness, almost an icy breath, emanated from her. Wherever she was, she brought a chill into the warm air. Later Paula was to remember this first impression and, in an agony of guilt, reproach herself for not warning her father, for not telling him of a wild premonition that was to prove justified. She did nothing. She went to her bedroom and fell into a heavy troubled sleep.

Jacqueline's reaction was very different. From having been violently opposed to engaging this woman, till then unseen, she did a complete about-face within two minutes. Two factors decided her, or rather her principal weaknesses decided for her. These were her vanity and her snobbishness.

She rose as the woman came into the room and held out her hand.

'Good afternoon. You're very punctual.'

'Good afternoon, madam.'

Except by assistants in the few remaining old-fashioned shops in Stantwich, Jacqueline hadn't been addressed as madam for many years. She was delighted. She smiled.

'Is it Miss Parchman or Mrs?'

'Miss Parchman. Eunice Parchman.'

'Won't you sit down?'

No repulsive chill or, as Melinda would have put it, 'vibes' affected Jacqueline. She was the last of the family to feel it, perhaps because she didn't want to, because almost from that

14

first moment she was determined to take Eunice Parchman on, and then, during the months that followed, to keep her. She saw a placid-looking creature with rather too small a head, pale firm features, brown hair mixed with grey, small steady blue eyes, a massive body that seemed neither to go out nor in, large shapely hands, very clean with short nails, large shapely legs in heavy brown nylon, large feet in somewhat distorted black court shoes. As soon as Eunice Parchman had sat down she undid the top button of her raincoat to disclose the polo neck of a lighter blue-ribbed jumper. Calmly she sat there, looking down at her hands folded in her lap.

Without admitting it even to herself, Jacqueline Coverdale liked handsome men and plain women. She got on well with Melinda but not so well as she got on with the less attractive Paula and Peter's *jolie laide* wife, Audrey. She suffered from what might be called a Gwendolen Complex, for like Wilde's Miss Fairfax, she preferred a woman to be 'fully forty-two and more than usually plain for her age'. Eunice Parchman was at least as old as herself, very likely older, though it was hard to tell, and there was no doubt about her plainness. If she had belonged to her own class, Jacqueline would have wondered why she didn't wear make-up, undergo a diet, have that tabby-cat hair tinted. But in a servant all was as it should be.

In the face of this respectful silence, confronted by this entirely prepossessing appearance, Jacqueline forgot the questions she had intended to ask. And instead of examining the candidate, instead of attempting to find out if this woman were suitable to work in her house, if she would suit the Coverdales, she began persuading Eunice Parchman that they would suit her.

'It's a big house, but there are only the three of us except when my stepdaughter comes home for the weekend. There's a cleaner three days a week, and of course I should do all the cooking myself.'

'I can cook, madam,' said Eunice.

'It wouldn't be necessary, really. There's a dishwasher and a deep-freeze. My husband and I do all the shopping.' Jacqueline was impressed by this woman's toneless voice that, though uneducated, had no trace of a cockney accent. 'We do entertain quite a lot,' she said almost fearfully.

Eunice moved her feet, bringing them close together. She nodded slowly. 'I'm used to that. I'm a hard worker.'

At this point Jacqueline should have asked why Eunice was leaving her present situation, or at least something about her present situation. For all she knew, there might not have been one. She didn't ask. She was bemused by those 'madams', excited by the contrast between this woman and Eva Baalham, this woman and the last pert too-pretty au pair. It was all so different from what she had expected.

Eagerly she said, 'When could you start?'

Eunice's blank face registered a faint surprise, as well it might.

'You'll want a reference,' she said.

'Oh, yes,' said Jacqueline, reminded. 'Of *course*.'

A white card was produced from Eunice's large black handbag. On it was written in the same handwriting as the letter that had so dismayed Jacqueline in the first place: Mrs Chichester, 24 Willow Vale, London, S.W. 18, and a phone number. The address was the one which had headed Eunice's letter.

'That's Wimbledon, isn't it?'

Eunice nodded. No doubt she was gladdened by this erroneous assumption. They discussed wages, when she would start, how she would travel to Stantwich. Subject, of course, Jacqueline said hastily, to the reference being satisfactory.

'I'm sure we shall get on marvellously.'

At last Eunice smiled. Her eyes remained cold and still, but her mouth moved. It was certainly a smile. 'Mrs Chichester said, could you phone her tonight before nine? She's an old lady and she goes to bed early.'

This show of tender regard for an employer's wishes and foibles could only be pleasing.

'You may be sure I shall,' said Jacqueline.

It was only twenty past two and the interview was over.

Eunice said, 'Thank you, madam. I can see myself out,' thus indicating, or so it seemed to Jacqueline, that she knew her place. She walked steadily from the room without looking back.

*

If Jacqueline had had a better knowledge of Greater London, she would have realized that Eunice Parchman had already told her a lie, or at least acquiesced in a misapprehension. For the postal district of Wimbledon is S.W. 19 not S.W. 18 which designates a much less affluent area in the Borough of Wandsworth. But she didn't realize and she didn't check, and when she entered Lowfield Hall at six, five minutes after George had got home, she didn't even show him the white card.

'I'm sure she'll be ideal, darling,' she enthused, 'really the kind of old-fashioned servant we thought was an extinct breed. I can't tell you how quiet and respectful she was, not a bit pushing. I'm only afraid she may be too humble. But I *know* she's going to be a hard worker.'

George put his arm round his wife and kissed her. He said nothing about her *volte face*, uttered no 'I told you so's'. He was accustomed to Jacqueline's prejudices, succeeded often by wild enthusiasm, and he loved her for her impulsiveness which, in his eyes made her seem young and sweet and feminine. What he said was, 'I don't care how humble she is or how pushing, as long as she takes some of the load of work off your hands.'

17

Before she made the phone call Jacqueline, who had an active imagination, had formed a picture in her mind of the kind of household in which Eunice Parchman worked and the kind of woman who employed her. Willow Vale, she thought, would be a quiet tree-lined road near Wimbledon Common number 24 large, Victorian; Mrs Chichester an elderly gentlewoman with rigid notions of behaviour, demanding but just, autocratic, whose servant was leaving her because she wouldn't, or couldn't afford to pay her adequate wages in these inflationary times.

At eight o'clock she dialled the number. Eunice Parchman answered the phone herself by giving the code correctly followed by the four digits slowly and precisely enunciated. Again calling Jacqueline madam, she asked her to hold the line while she fetched Mrs Chichester. And Jacqueline imagined her crossing a sombre over-furnished hall, entering a large and rather chilly drawing room where an old lady sat listening to classical music or reading the In Memoriam column in a quality newspaper. There, on the threshold, she would pause and say in her deferential way:

'Mrs Coverdale on the phone for you, madam.'

The facts were otherwise.

The telephone in question was attached to the wall on the first landing of a rooming house in Earlsfield, at the top of a flight of stairs. Eunice Parchman had been waiting patiently by it since five in case, when it rang, some other tenant should get to it first. Mrs Chichester was a machine-tool operator in her fifties called Annie Cole who sometimes performed small services of this kind in exchange for Eunice agreeing not to tell the Post Office how, for a year after her mother's death, she had continued to draw that lady's pension. Annie had written the letter and the words on the card, and it was from her furnished room, number 6, 24 Willow Vale, S.W. 18, that Eunice now fetched her to the phone. Annie Cole said:

'I'm really very upset to be losing Miss Parchman, Mrs Coverdale. She's managed everything so wonderfully for me for seven years. She's a marvellous worker, and excellent cook, and so house-proud! Really, if she has a fault, it's that she's too conscientious.'

Even Jacqueline felt that this was laying it on a bit thick. And the voice was peculiarly sprightly – Annie Cole couldn't get rid of Eunice fast enough – with an edge to it the reverse of refined. She had the sense to ask why this paragon was leaving.

'Because I'm leaving myself.' The reply came without hesitation. 'I'm joining my son in New Zealand. The cost of living is getting impossible here, isn't it? Miss Parchman could come with me, I should welcome the idea, but she's rather conservative. She prefers to stay here. I should like to think of her settling in a nice family like yours.'

Jacqueline was satisfied.

'Did you confirm it with Miss Parchman?' said George.

'Oh, darling, I forgot. I'll have to write to her.'

'Or phone back.'

Why not phone back, Jacqueline? Dial that number again now. A young man returning to his room next to Annie Cole's, setting his foot now on the last step of that flight of stairs, will lift the receiver. And when you ask for Miss Parchman he will tell you he has never heard of her. Mrs Chichester, then? There is no Mrs Chichester, only a Mr Chichester who is the landlord, in whose name the phone number is but who himself lives in Croydon. Pick up the phone now, Jacqueline...

'I think it's better to confirm it in writing.'

Just as you like, darling.'

The moment passed, the chance was lost. George did pick up the phone, but it was to call Paula, for the report on her health he had received from his wife had disquieted him. While he was talking to her, Jacqueline wrote her letter.

19

And the other people whom chance and destiny and their own agency were to bring together for destruction on 14 February? Joan Smith was preaching on a cottage doorstep. Melinda Coverdale, in her room in Galwich, was struggling to make sense out of *Sir Gawain and the Green Knight*. Giles Mont was reciting mantras as an aid to meditation.

But already they were gathered together. In that moment when Jacqueline declined to make a phone call an invisible thread lassoed each of them, bound them one to another, related them more closely than blood.

Chapter 3

George and Jacqueline were discreet people, and they didn't broadcast their coming good fortune. But Jacqueline did mention it to her friend Lady Royston who mentioned it to Mrs Cairne when the eternal subject of getting someone to keep the place clean came up. The news seeped through along the ramifications of Higgses, Meadowses, Baalhams and Newsteads, and in the Blue Boar it succeeded as the major topic of conversation over the latest excesses of Joan Smith.

Eva Baalham hastened, in her oblique way, to let Jacqueline know that she knew. 'You going to give her telly?'

'Give whom – er, television?' said Jacqueline flushing.

'Her as is coming from London. Because if you are I can as like get you a set cheap from my cousin Meadows as has the electric shop in Gosbury. Fell off the back of a lorry, I reckon, but ask no questions and you'll get no lies.'

'Thank you so much,' said Jacqueline, more than a little annoyed. 'As a matter of fact, we're buying a colour set for ourselves and Miss Parchman will be having our old one.'

'Parchman,' said Eva, spitting on a window-pane before giving it a wipe with her apron. 'Would that be a London name, I wonder?'

'I really don't know, Mrs Baalham. When you've finished whatever you're doing to that window perhaps you'd be good enough to come upstairs with me and we'll start getting her room ready.'

'I reckon,' said Eva in her broad East Anglian whine. She

never called Jacqueline madam; it wouldn't have crossed her mind. In her eyes, the only difference between herself and the Coverdales was one of money. In other respects she was their superior since they were newcomers, and not even gentry but in trade, while her yeomen ancestors had lived in Greeving for five hundred years. Nor did she envy them their money. She had quite enough of her own, and she preferred her council house to Lowfield Hall, great big barn of a place, must cost a packet keeping that warm. She didn't like Jacqueline, who was mutton dressed as lamb and who gave herself some mighty airs for the wife of the owner of a tin-can factory. All that will-you-be-so-good and thank-you-so-much nonsense. Wonder how she'll get on with this Parchman? Wonder how I will? Still, I reckon I can always leave. There's Mrs Jameson-Kerr begging me to come on her bended knees and she'll pay sixty pence an hour.

'God help her legs,' said Eva, mounting the stairs.

At the top of the house a warren of poky attics had long since been converted into two large bedrooms and a bathroom. From their windows could be seen one of the finest pastoral views in East Anglia. Constable, of course, had painted it, sitting on the banks of the River Beal, and as was sometimes his way he had shifted a few church towers the better to suit his composition. It was lovely enough with the church towers in their proper places, a wide serene view of meadows and little woods in all the delicious varied greens of early May.

'Have her bed in here, will she?' said Eva, ambling into the bigger and sunnier of the bedrooms.

'No, she won't.' Jacqueline could see that Eva was preparing to line herself up as secretary, as it were, of the downtrodden domestic servants' union. 'I want that room for when my husband's grandchildren come to stay.'

'You'll have to make her comfortable if you want her to stop.' Eva opened a window. 'Lovely day. Going to be a hot summer. The Lord is on our side, as my cousin as has the farm

22

always says. There's young Giles going off in your car without so much as by your leave, I reckon.'

Jacqueline was furious. She thought Eva ought to call Giles Mr Mont or, at least, 'your son'. But she was glad to see Giles, who was on half-term, leave his voluntary incarceration at last to get some fresh air.

'If you'd be so kind, Mrs Baalham, we might start moving the furniture.'

Giles drove down the avenue between the horsechestnut trees and out into Greeving Lane. The lane is an unclassified road, just wide enough for two cars to pass if they go very slowly. Blackthorn had given place to hawthorn, and the hedges were creamy with its sugary scented blossom. A limped blue sky, pale green wheat growing, a cuckoo calling – in May he sings all day – an exultation of birds carolling their territorial claims from every tree.

Pretending that none of it was there, refusing, in spite of his creed, to be one with the oneness of it, Giles drove over the river bridge. He intended to get as little fresh air as was compatible with going out of doors. He loathed the country. It bored him. There was nothing to do. When you told people that they were shocked, presumably because they didn't realize that no one in his senses could spend more than a maximum of an hour a day looking at the stars, walking in the fields or sitting on river banks. Besides, it was nearly always cold or muddy. He disliked shooting things or fishing things out of streams or riding horses or following the hunt. George, who had tried to encourage him in those pursuits, had perhaps at last understood the impossibility of the task. Giles never, but *never,* went for a country walk. When he was compelled to walk to Lowfield Hall from the point where the school bus stopped, about half a mile, he kept his eyes on the ground. He had tried shutting them, but he had bumped into a tree.

London he loved. Looking back, he thought he had been happy in London. He had wanted to go to a boarding school in a big city, but his mother hadn't let him because some psychologist had said he was disturbed and needed the secure background of family life. Being disturbed didn't bother him, and he rather fostered the air he had of the absent-minded, scatty, preoccupied young intellectual. He was intellectual all right, very much so. Last year he had got so many O-levels that there had been a piece about him in a national newspaper. He was certain of a place at Oxford, and he knew as much Latin, and possibly more Greek, than the man who professed to teach him these subjects at the Magnus Wythen.

He had no friends at school, and he despised the village boys who were interested only in motorcycles, pornography and the Blue Boar. Ian and Christopher Cairne and others of their like had been designated his friends by parental edict, but he hardly ever saw them, as they were away at their public schools. Neither the village boys nor those at school ever attempted to beat him up. He was over six feet and still growing. His face was horrible with acne, and the day after he washed it his hair was again wet with grease.

Now he was on his way to Sudbury to buy a packet of orange dye. He was going to dye all his jeans and tee-shirts orange in pursuance of his religion, which was, roughly, Buddhism. When he had saved up enough money he meant to go to India on a bus and, with the exception of Melinda, never see any of them again. Well, maybe his mother. But not his father or stuffy old George or self-righteous Peter or this bunch of peasants. That is, if he didn't become a Catholic instead. He had just finished reading *Brideshead Revisited,* and had begun to wonder whether being a Catholic at Oxford and burning incense on one's staircase might not be better than India. But he'd dye the jeans and tee-shirts just in case.

At Meadows' garage in Greeving he stopped for petrol.

'When's the lady from London coming, then?' said Jim Meadows.

'Mmm?' said Giles.

Jim wanted to know so that he could tell them in the pub that night. He tried again. Giles thought about it reluctantly. 'Is today Wednesday?'

''Course it is.' Jim added, because he fancied himself as a wit, 'All day.'

'They said Saturday,' said Giles at last. 'I think.'

It might be and it might not, thought Jim. You never knew with him. Needed his head seeing to that one. It was a wonder she let him out alone at the wheel of a good car like that. 'Melinda'll be home to get a look at her, I reckon.'

'Mmm,' said Giles. He drove off, rejecting the green stamps.

Melinda would be home. He didn't know whether this was pleasing or disquieting. On the surface, his relationship with her was casual and even distant, but in Giles's heart, where he often saw himself as a Poe or Byron, it simmered as an incestuous passion. This had come into being, or been pushed into being, by Giles six months before. Until then Melinda had merely been a kind of quasi-sister. He knew, of course, that since she was not his sister, or even his half-sister, there was nothing at all to stop their falling in love with each other and eventually marrying. Apart from the three years' age difference, which would be of no importance later on, there could be no possible objection on anyone's part. Mother would even like it and old George would come round. But this was not what Giles wanted or what he saw in his fantasies. In them Melinda and he were a Byron and an Augusta Leigh who confessed their mutual passion while walking in Wuthering Heights weather on the Greeving Hills, a pastime which nothing would have induced Giles to undertake in reality. There was little reality in any of this. In his fantasies Melinda even looked different, paler, thinner, rather phthisic, very much of another world. Confronting each other, breathless in the windswept darkness, they spoke of how their love must remain for ever secret, never of course to be consummated. And though they married other people, their passion endured and was whispered of as something profound and indefinable.

He bought the dye, two packets of it called Nasturtium Flame. He also bought a poster of a PreRaphaelite girl with a pale green face and red hair, hanging over a balcony. The girl was presumably craning out of her window to moon after a lost or faithless lover, but from her attitude and the nauseous pallor of her skin she looked more as if, while staying in an hotel in an Italian holiday resort, she had eaten too much pasta and was going to be sick. Giles bought her because she looked like Melinda would look in the terminal stages of tuberculosis.

He returned to the car to find a parking ticket on the windscreen. He never used the car park. It would have meant walking a hundred yards. When he got home Eva had gone and so had his mother, who had left a note on the kitchen table for him. The note began 'Darling' and ended 'love from Mother' and the middle was full of needless information about the cold lunch left for him in the fridge and how she had had to go to some Women's Institute meeting. It mystified him. He knew where his lunch would be, and he would never have dreamed of leaving a note for anyone. Like all true eccentrics, he thought other people very odd.

Presently he fetched all his clothes downstairs and put them with the dye and some water in the two large pans his mother used for jam-making. While they were boiling, he sat at the kitchen table eating chicken salad and reading the memoirs of a mystic who had lived in a Poona Ashram for thirty years without speaking a word.

On the Friday afternoon Melinda Coverdale came home. The

train brought her from Galwich to Stantwich, and the bus to a place called Gallows Corner two miles from Lowfield Hall. There she alighted and waited for a lift. At this hour there was always someone passing on his or her way home to Greeving, so Melinda hoisted herself up on to Mrs Cotleigh's garden wall and sat in the sun.

She was wearing over-long jeans rolled up to the knees, very scuffed red cowboy boots, an Indian cotton shirt and a yellow motoring hat, vintage 1920. But for all that there was no prettier sight to be seen on a sunny garden wall between Stantwich and King's Lynn. Melinda was the child who had inherited George's looks. She had his straight nose and high brow, his sharply sensitive mouth and his bright blue eyes – and her dead mother's mane of golden hair, the colour of Mrs Cotleigh's wallflowers.

An energy that never seemed to flag, except where Middle English verse was concerned, kept her constantly on the move. She lugged her horse's nosebag holdall up on to the wall beside her, pulled out a string of beads, tried it on, made a face at the textbooks which hope rather than incentive had persuaded her to bring, then flung the bag down on the grass and jumped after it. Cross-legged on the bank while the useless bus passed in the opposite direction, then to pick poppies, the wild red poppies, weeds of Suffolk, that abound on this corner where once the gibbet stood.

Five minutes later the chicken-farm van came along, and Geoff Baalham, who was second cousin to Eva called, 'Hi, Melinda! Can I drop you?'

She jumped in, hat, bag and poppies. 'I must have been there half an hour,' said Melinda, who had been there ten minutes.

'I like your hat.'

'Do you really, Geoff? You are *sweet*. I got it in the Oxfam shop.' Melinda knew everyone in the village and called everyone, even ancient gaffers and gammers, by their Christian names. She drove tractors and picked fruit and watched calvings. In the presence of her father she spoke more or less politely to Jameson-Kerrs, Archers, Cairnes and Sir Robert Royston, but she disapproved of them as reactionary. Once, when the foxhounds had met on Greeving Green, she had gone up there waving an anti-bloodsports banner. In her early teens she had gone fishing with the village boys and with them watched the hares come out at dusk. In her late teens she had danced with them at Cattingham 'hops' and kissed them behind the village hall. She was as gossipy as their mothers and as involved.

'What's been going on in merry old Greeving in my absence? Tell all.' She hadn't been home for three weeks. 'I know, Mrs Archer's eloped with Mr Smith.'

Geoff Baalham grinned widely. 'Poor old sod. I reckon he's got his hands full with his own missus. Wait a minute, let's see. Susan Meadows, Higgs that was, had her baby. It's a girl, and they're calling it Lalage.'

'You don't *mean* it!'

'Thought that'd shake you. Your ma's got herself on the parish council, though I reckon you know about that, and – wait for it – your dad's bought colour telly.'

'I talked to him on the phone last night. He never said.'

'No, well, only got it today. I had it all from my Auntie Eva an hour back.' The people of Greeving are careless about the correct terms for relations. One's stepmother is as much one's ma or mum as one's natural mother, and a female second cousin, if old enough, is necessarily auntie. 'They're giving the old one to the lady help that's coming from London.'

'Oh God, how; mean! Daddy's such a ghastly fascist. Don't you think that's the most undemocratic fascist thing you've ever heard, Geoff?'

'It's the way of the world, Melinda, love. Always has been and always will be. You oughtn't to go calling your dad names. I'd turn you over and tan your backside for you if I was him.'

'Geoff Baalham! To hear you, no one'd think you're only a year older than me.'

'Just you remember I'm a married man now, and that teaches you the meaning of responsibility. Here we are, Low-field Hall, madame, and I'll take my leave of you. Oh, and you can tell your ma I'll be sending them eggs up with Auntie Eva first thing Monday morning.'

'Will do. Thanks tremendously for the lift, Geoff. You are *sweet*.'

'Cheerio then, Melinda.'

Off went Geoff to the chicken farm and Barbara Carter whom he had married in January, but thinking what a nice pretty girl Melinda Coverdale was – that hat, my God! – and thinking too of walking with her years before by the River Beal and of innocent kisses exchanged to the rushing music of the mill.

Melinda swung up the long drive, under the chestnuts hung with their cream and bronze candles, round the house and in by the gun-room door. Giles was sitting at the kitchen table reading the last chapter of the Poona book.

'Hi, Step.'

'Hallo,' said Giles. He no longer used the nickname that once had served for each to address to the other. It was incongruous with his Byronic fantasies, though these always crumbled when Melinda appeared in the flesh. She had quite a lot of well-distributed flesh, and red cheeks, and an aggressive healthiness. Also she bounced. Giles sighed, scratched his spots and thought of being in India with a begging bowl.

'How did you get red ink on your jeans?'

'I didn't. I've dyed them but the dye didn't take.'

'Mad,' said Melinda. She sailed off, searched for her father and stepmother, found them on the top floor putting finishing touches to Miss Parchman's room. 'Hallo, my darlings.'

Each got a kiss, but George got his first. 'Daddy, you've got a suntan. If I'd known you were coming home so early I'd have phoned your office from the station. Geoff Baalham gave me a lift and he said his Auntie Eva'll bring the eggs first thing on Monday and you're giving our new housekeeper the old telly. I said I never heard anything so fascist in all my life. Next thing you'll be saying she's got to eat on her own in the kitchen.'

George and Jacqueline looked at each other.

'Well, of course.'

'How awful! No wonder the revolution's coming. *A bas les aristos.* D'you like my hat, Jackie? I bought it in the Oxfam shop. Fifty pee. God, I'm *starving.* We haven't got anyone awful coming tonight, have we? No curs or cairns or roisterers?'

'Now, Melinda, I think that's enough.' The words were admonitory but the tone was tender. George was incapable of being really cross with his favourite child. 'We're tolerant of your friends and you must be tolerant of ours. As a matter of fact, the Roystons are dining with us.'

Melinda groaned. Quickly she hugged her father before he could expostulate. 'I shall go and phone Stephen or Charles or someone and *make* him take me out. But I tell you what, Jackie, I'll be back in time to help you clear up. Just think, you'll never have to do it again after tomorrow when Parchment Face comes.'

'Melinda...' George began.

'She had got rather a parchment look to her face,' said Jacqueline, and she couldn't help laughing.

So Melinda went to the cinema in Nunchester with Stephen Crutchley, the doctor's son. The Roystons came to dine at Lowfield Hall, and Jacqueline said, Wait till tomorrow. Don't you envy me, Jessica? But what will she be like? And will she really come up to these glowing expectations? It was George who wondered. Please God, let her be the treasure Jackie thinks she is. *Schadenfreude* made Sir Robert and Lady Royston secretly hope she wouldn't be, but cut on the same lines as their Anneliese, their Birgit and that best-forgotten Spanish couple.

Time will show. Wait till tomorrow.

Chapter 4

The Coverdales had speculated about Eunice Parchman as to her work potential and her attitude, respectful or otherwise, towards themselves. They had allotted her a private bathroom and a television set, some comfortable chairs and a well-sprung bed rather as one sees that a workhorse has a good stable and manger. They wanted her to be content because if she were contented she would stay. But they never considered her as a person at all. Not for them as they got up on Saturday, 9 May, E-Day indeed, any thoughts as to what her past had been, whether she was nervous about coming, whether she was visited by the same hopes and fears that affected them. At that stage Eunice was little more than a machine to them, and the satisfactory working of that machine depended on its being suitably oiled and its having no objection to stairs.

But Eunice was a person. Eunice, as Melinda might have put it, was for real.

She was the strangest person they were ever likely to meet. And had they known what her past contained, they would have fled from her or barred their doors against her as against the plague – not to mention her future, now inextricably bound up with theirs.

Her past lay in the house she was now preparing to leave; an old terraced house, one of a long row in Rainbow Street, Tooting, with its front door opening directly on to the pavement. She had been born in that house, forty-seven years before, the only child of a Southern Railway guard and his wife.

From the first her existence was a narrow one. She seemed one of those people who are destined to spend their lives in the restricted encompassment of a few streets. Her school was almost next door, Rainbow Street Infants, and those members of her family she visited lived within a stone's throw. Destiny was temporarily disturbed by the coming of the Second World War. Along with thousands of other London schoolchildren, she was sent away to the country before she had learned to read. But her parents, though dull, unaware, mole-like people, were upset by reports that her foster mother neglected her, and fetched her back to them, to the bombs and the war-torn city.

After that Eunice attended school only sporadically. To this school or that school she went for weeks or sometimes months at a time, but in each new class she entered the other pupils were all far ahead of her. They had passed her by, and no teacher ever took the trouble to discover the fundamental gap in her acquirements, still less to remedy it. Bewildered, bored, apathetic, she sat at the back of the classroom, staring at the incomprehensible on page or blackboard. Or she stayed away, a stratagem always connived at by her mother. Therefore, by the time she came to leave school a month before her fourteenth birthday, she could sign her name, read 'The cat sat on the mat' and 'Jim likes ham but Jack likes jam', and that was about all. School had taught her one thing – to conceal, by many subterfuges and contrivances, that she could not read or write.

She went to work in a sweetshop, also in Rainbow Street, where she learned to tell a Mars bar from a Crunchie by the colour of its wrapping. When she was seventeen, the illness which had threatened her mother for years began to cripple her. It was multiple sclerosis, though it was some time before the Parchmans' doctor understood this. Mrs Parchman, at fifty, was confined to a wheelchair, and Eunice gave up her job to look after her and run the house. Her days now began to be spent in a narrow twilight world, for illiteracy is a kind of blindness. The Coverdales, had they been told of it, would not have believed such a world could exist. Why didn't she educate herself? They would have asked. Why didn't she go to evening classes, get a job, employ someone to look after her mother, join a club, meet people? Why, indeed. Between the Coverdales and the Parchmans a great gulf is fixed. George himself often said so, without fully considering what it implied. A young girl to him was always some version of Paula or Melinda, cherished, admired, educated, loved, brought up to see herself as one of the top ten per cent. Not so Eunice Parchman. A big raw-boned plain girl with truculent sullen eyes, she had never heard a piece of music except for the hymns and the extracts from Gilbert and Sullivan her father whistled while he shaved. She had never seen any picture of note but 'The Laughing Cavalier' and the 'Mona Lisa' in the school hall, and she was so steeped in ignorance that had you asked her who Napoleon was and where was Denmark, she would have stared in uncomprehending blankness.

There were things Eunice could do. She had considerable manual dexterity. She could clean expertly and shop and cook and sew and push her mother up to the common in her wheelchair. Was it so surprising that, being able to do these things, she should prefer the safety and peace of doing them and them alone? Was it odd to find her taking satisfaction in gossiping with her middle-aged neighbours and avoiding the company of their children who could read and write and who had jobs and talked of things beyond her comprehension? She had her pleasures, eating the chocolate she loved and which made her grow stout, ironing, cleaning silver and brass, augmenting the family income by knitting for her neighbours. By the time she was thirty she had never been into a public house, visited a theatre, entered any restaurant more grand than a teashop, left the country, had a boyfriend, worn make-up or been to a hairdresser. She had twice been to the cinema with Mrs Samson next door and had seen the Queen's wedding and coronation on Mrs Samson's television set. Between the ages of seven and twelve she four times travelled in a long-distance train. That was the history of her youth.

Virtue might naturally be the concomitant of such sheltering. She had few opportunities to do bad things, but she found them or made them.

'If there's one thing I've taught Eunice,' her mother used to say, 'it's to tell right from wrong.' It was a gabbled cliché, as automatic as the quacking of a duck but less meaningful. The Parchmans were not given to thinking before they spoke, or indeed to thinking much at all.

All that jerked Eunice out of her apathy were her compulsions. Suddenly an urge would come over her to drop everything and walk. Or turn out a room. Or take a dress to pieces and sew it up again with minor alterations. These urges she always obeyed. Buttoned up tightly into her shabby coat, a scarf tied round her still beautiful thick brown hair, she would walk and walk for miles, sometimes across the river bridges and up into the West End. These walks were her education. She saw things one is not taught in school even if one can read. And instincts, not controlled or repressed by reading, instructed her as to what these sights meant or implied. In the West End she saw prostitutes, in the park people making love, on the commons homosexuals waiting furtively in the shadows to solicit likely passers-by. One night she saw a man who lived in Rainbow Street pick up a boy and take him behind a bush. Eunice had never heard the word blackmail. She didn't know that demanding money with menaces is a popular pastime punishable by the law. But neither, probably, had Cain heard the word murder before he struck his brother down. There are age-old desires in man which man needs no instruction to practise. Very likely

Eunice thought she was doing something original. She waited until the boy had gone and then she told her neighbour she would tell his wife unless he gave her ten shillings a week not to do so. Horribly frightened, he agreed and gave her ten shillings a week for years.

Her father had been religious in his youth. He named her after a New Testament character, and sometimes, facetiously, would refer to this fact, pronouncing her name in the Greek way.

'What have you got for my tea tonight, Eu-nicey, mother of Timothy?'

It riled Eunice. It rankled. Did she vaguely ponder on the likelihood that she would never be the mother of anyone? The thoughts of the illiterate are registered in pictures and in very simple words. Eunice's vocabulary was small. She spoke in clichés and catch-phrases picked up from her mother, and her aunt down the road, Mrs Samson. When her cousin married, did she feel envy? Was there bitterness as well as greed in her heart when she began extracting a further ten shillings a week from a married woman who was having an affair with a salesman? She expressed to no one her emotions or her views on life.

Mrs Parchman died when Eunice was thirty-seven, and her widower immediately took over as resident invalid. Perhaps he thought Eunice's services too good to waste. His kidneys had always been weak, and now he cultivated his asthma, taking to his bed.

'I don't know where I'd be without you, Eu-nicey, mother of Timothy.'

Alive today, probably, and living in Tooting.

Eunice's urges pressed her one day to get on a coach and have a day in Brighton, another to take all the furniture out of the living room and paint the walls pink. Her father went into hospital for the odd fortnight.

'Mainly to give you a break, Miss Parchman,' said the doctor. 'He could go at any time, he could last for years.'

But he showed no signs of going. Eunice bought him nice bits of fish and made him steak and kidney pudding. She kept up his bedroom fire and brought him hot water to shave in while he whistled 'The King of Love my Shepherd is' and 'I am the Lord High Executioner'. One bright morning in spring he sat up in bed, pink-cheeked and strong, and said in the clear voice of one whose lungs are perfectly sound:

'You can wrap me up warm and put me in Mum's chair and take me up on the common, Eu-nicey mother of Timothy.'

Eunice made no reply. She took one of the pillows from behind her father's head and pushed it hard down on his face. He struggled and thrashed about for a while, but not for long. His lungs, after all, were not quite sound. Eunice had no phone. She walked up the street and brought the doctor back with her. He asked no questions and signed the death certificate at once.

Now for freedom.

She was forty, and she didn't know what to do with freedom now that she had it. Get over that ridiculous business of not being able to read and write, George Coverdale would have said. Learn a useful trade. Take in lodgers. Get some sort of social life going. Eunice did none of these things. She remained in the house in Rainbow Street, for which the rent was scarcely now more than nominal, and she had her black-mail income, swollen now to two pounds a week. As if those twenty-three years had never been, those best years of all her youth passed as in the twinkling of an eye, she went back to the sweetshop and worked there three days a week.

On one of her walks she saw Annie Cole go into a post office in Merton with a pension book in her hand. Eunice knew a pension book when she saw one. She had been shown by her father how to sign his as his agent. And she knew Annie Cole by sight too, having observed her leaving the crematorium just before Mr Parchman's funeral party had arrived. It was Annie Cole's mother who had died, and now here was Annie Cole collecting her pension and telling the counter clerk how poor mother had rallied that day. The advantage of being illiterate is that one achieves an excellent visual memory and almost total recall.

Annie thereby became Eunice's victim and amanuensis, paying her a third of that pension and doing needful jobs for her. She also, because she bore no malice, seeing Eunice's conduct as only natural in a catch-as-catch-can world, became the nearest Eunice ever had to a friend until she met Joan Smith. But it was time now to kill Mother off finally as she was getting scared, only Eunice as beneficiary wouldn't let her. She determined to be rid of Eunice, and it was she who, having flattered her blackmailer to the top of her bent on her housewifely skills produced as if casually the Coverdales' advertisement.

'You could get thirty-five pounds a week and all found. I've always said you were wasted in that shop.'

Eunice munched her Cadbury's filled block. 'I don't know,' she said, a favourite response.

'That place of yours is falling down. They're always talking about pulling that row down. It'd be no loss, I'm sure.' Annie scrutinized *The Times* which she had picked at random out of a litter bin. 'It sounds ever so nice. Why not write to them and just see? You don't have to go there if you don't fancy it.'

'You can write if you want,' said Eunice.

Like all her close acquaintances, Annie suspected Eunice was illiterate or semi-literate, but no one could ever be quite sure. Eunice sometimes seemed to read magazines, and she could sign things. There are many people, after all, who never read or write although they can. So Annie wrote the letter to Jacqueline, and when the time came for the interview it was Annie who primed Eunice.

'Be sure to call her madam, Eun, and don't speak till you're spoken to. Mother was in service when she was a girl and she knew all about it. I can give you a good many of Mother's tips.' Poor Annie. She had been devoted to her mother, and the pension-book fraud had been perpetrated as much as a way of keeping her mother alive and with her as for gain. 'You can have a lend of Mother's court shoes too. They'll be about your size.'

It worked. Before Eunice could think much about it, she was engaged as the Coverdales' housekeeper, and if it was at twenty-five rather than thirty-five pounds a week, either seemed a fortune to her. And yet, why was she so easily persuaded, she who was as bound to her burrow and her warren as any wild animal?

Not for pastures new, adventure, pecuniary advantage, or even the chance of showing off the one thing she could do well. Largely, she took the job to avoid responsibility.

While her father was alive, though things had been bad in many respects, they had been good in one. He took responsibility for the rent and the rates and the services bills, for filling in forms and reading what had to be read. Eunice took the rates round to the council offices in cash, paid the gas and electricity bills in the same way. But she couldn't hire television or buy it on HP – there would have been forms to fill in. Letters and circulars came; she couldn't read them. Lowfield Hall would solve all that, and as far as she could see, receive her and care for her in the only way she was interested in for ever.

The house was rendered up to an amazed and delighted landlord, and Mrs Samson saw to the selling of the furniture. Eunice watched the valuing of her household goods, and the indifference on the man's face, with an inscrutable expression. She packed everything she possessed into two suitcases, borrowed from Mrs Samson. In her blue skirt, handknitted blue

39

jumper, and navy raincoat she made, characteristically, her farewells to that kind neighbour, that near-mother who had been present when her own mother gave her birth.

'Well, I'm off,' said Eunice.

Mrs Samson kissed her cheek, but she didn't ask Eunice to write to her, for she was the only living person who really knew.

At Liverpool Street Station Eunice regarded trains – trains proper, not tubes – for the first time in nearly forty years. But how to find which one to take? On the departure board, white on black, were meaningless hieroglyphs.

She hated asking questions, but she had to.

'Which platforms for Stantwich?'

'It's up on the board, lady.'

And again, to someone else. 'Which platform for Stantwich?'

'It's up on the board. Thirteen. Can't you read?'

No, she couldn't, but she didn't dare say so. Still, at last she was on the train, and it must be the right one, for by now eleven people had told her so. The train took her out into the country and back into the past. She was a little girl again, going with her school to Taunton and safety, and her whole future was before her. Now, as then, the stations passed, nameless and unknown.

But she would know Stantwich when she got there, for the train and her future went no further.

Chapter 5

She was bound to fail. She had no training and no experience. People like the Coverdales were far removed from any people she had ever known, and she was not accommodating or adaptable. She had never been to a party, let alone given one, never run any house but the one in Rainbow Street. There was no tradition of service in her family and no one she knew had ever had a servant, not even a charwoman. It was on the cards that she would fail abysmally.

She succeeded beyond her own stolid hopes and Jacqueline's dreams.

Of course, Jacqueline didn't really want a housekeeper at all. She didn't want an organizer and manager but an obedient maid of all work. And Eunice was accustomed to obedience and hard work. She was what the Coverdales required, apparently without personality or awareness of her rights or that curiosity that leads an employee to pry, quiet and respectable, not paranoid except in one particular, lacking any desire to put herself on the same social level as they. Aesthetic appreciation for her was directed to only one end – domestic objects. To Eunice a refrigerator was beautiful while a flower was just a flower, the fabric of a curtain lovely whereas a bird or a wild animal at best 'pretty'. She was unable to differentiate, as far as its aesthetic value was concerned, between a *famille rose* vase and a Teflon-lined frying pan. Both were 'nice' and each would receive from her the same care and attention.

These were the reasons for her success. From the first she

made a good impression. Having eaten the last of the Bounty bar she had bought herself at Liverpool Street, she alighted from the train, no longer nervous now that there was nothing to be deciphered. She could read Way Out, that wasn't a problem. Jacqueline hadn't told her how she would know George, but George knew her from his wife's not very kind description. Melinda was with him which had floored Eunice who was looking for a man on his own.

'Pleased to meet you,' she said, shaking hands, not smiling or studying them, but observing the big white car.

George gave her the front seat. 'You'll get a better view of our beautiful countryside that way, Miss Parchman.'

The girl chattered nineteen to the dozen all the way, occasionally shooting questions at Eunice. D'you like the country, Miss Parchman? Have you ever been up in the Fens? Aren't you too hot in that coat? I hope you like stuffed vine leaves. My stepmother's doing them for tonight. Eunice answered bemusedly with a plain yes or no. She didn't know whether you ate stuffed vine leaves or looked at them or sat on them. But she responded with quiet politeness, sometimes giving her a small tight smile.

George liked this respectful discretion. He liked the way she sat with her knees together and her hands folded in her lap. He even liked her clothes which to a more detached observer would have looked like standard issue to prison wardresses. Neither he nor Melinda was aware of anything chilly or repulsive about her.

'Go the long way round through Greeving, Daddy, so that Miss Parchman can see the village.'

It was thus that Eunice was given a view of her future accomplice's home before she saw that of her victims. Greeving Post Office and Village Store, Prop. N. Smith. She didn't, however, see Joan Smith, who was out delivering Epiphany People literature.

But she wouldn't have taken much notice of her if she had

42

been there. People didn't interest her. Nor did the country-side and one of the prettiest villages in Suffolk. Greeving was just old buildings to her, thatch and plaster and a lot of trees that must keep out the light. But she did wonder how you managed when you wanted a nice bit of fish or suddenly had a fancy, as she often did, for a pound box of chocolates.

Lowfield Hall. To Eunice it might have been Buckingham Palace. She didn't know ordinary people lived in houses like this which were for the Queen or some film star. In the hall, all five of them were together for the first time. Jacqueline, who dressed up for any occasion, got into emerald velvet trousers and red silk shirt and Gucci scarf to greet her new servant. Even Giles was there. Passing through at that particular moment, looking vaguely for his Hindi primer, he had been collared by his mother and persuaded to remain for an introduction.

'Good evening, Miss Parchman. Did you have a good journey? This is my son, Giles.'

Giles nodded absently and escaped upstairs without a backward glance. Eunice hardly noticed him. She was looking at the house and its contents. It was almost too much for her. She was like the Queen of Sheba when she saw King Solomon – there was no more spirit in her. But none of her wonderment showed in her face or her demeanour. She stood on the thick carpet, among the antiques, the bowls of flowers, looking first at the grandfather clock, then at herself reflected in a huge mirror with gilded twirls round the edge of it. She stood half-stunned. The Coverdales took her air for poise, the silent selfsufficient containment of the good servant.

'I'll take you to your room,' said Jacqueline. 'There won't be anything for you to do tonight. We'll go upstairs and someone will bring your bags up later.'

A large and pleasant room met Eunice's eyes. It was carpeted in olive drab Wilton, papered in a pale yellow with a white vertical stripe. There were two darker yellow easy chairs, a cretonne-covered settee, a bed with a spread of the same material and a long built-in cupboard. The windows afforded a splendid view, *the* view, which was better seen from here than from any other room in the house.

'I hope you find everything to your liking.'

An empty bookcase (destined to remain so), a bowl of white lilac on a coffee table, two lamps with burnt orange shades, two framed Constable reproductions, 'Willy Lott's Cottage' and 'The Leaping Horse'. The bathroom had light green fittings and olive green towels hung on a heated rail.

'Your dinner will be ready for you in the kitchen in half an hour. It's the door at the end of the passage behind the stairs. And now I expect you'd like to be left alone for a while. Oh, here's my son with your bags.'

Giles had been caught by George and coaxed into bringing up the two cases. He dumped them on the floor and went away. Eunice disregarded him as she had largely disregarded his mother. She was staring at the one object in those two rooms which really interested her, the television set. This was what she had always wanted but been unable to buy or hire. As the door closed behind Jacqueline, she approached the set, looked at it, and then, like someone resolved upon using a dangerous piece of equipment that may explode or send a shock up one's arm, but knowing still that it must be used, it must be attempted, she pounced on it and switched it on.

On the screen appeared a man with a gun. He was threatening a woman who cowered behind a chair. There was a shot and the woman fled screaming down a corridor. Thus it happened that the first programme Eunice ever saw on her own television dealt with violence and with firearms. Did it and its many successors stimulate her own latent violence and trigger off waves of aggression? Did fictional drama take root in the mind of the illiterate so that it at last bore terrible fruit?

Perhaps. But if television spurred her on to kill the Coverdales it certainly played no part in directing her to smother her father. At the time of his death the only programmes she had seen on it were a royal wedding and a coronation.

However, though she was to become addicted to the set, shutting herself up with it and drawing her curtains against the summer evenings, that first time she watched it for only ten minutes. She ate her dinner cautiously, for it was like nothing she had ever eaten before, and was taken over the house by Jacqueline, instructed in her duties. From the very beginning she enjoyed herself. A few little mistakes were only natural. Annie Cole had taught her how to lay a table, so she did that all right, but on that first morning she made tea instead of coffee. Eunice had never made coffee in her life except the instant kind. She didn't ask how. She very seldom asked questions. Jacqueline assumed she was used to a percolator – Eunice didn't disillusion her – while they used a filter, so she demonstrated the filter. Eunice watched. It was never necessary for her to watch any operation of this kind more than once for her to be able to perform it herself.

'I see, madam,' she said.

Jacqueline did the cooking. Jacqueline or George did the shopping. In those early days, while Jacqueline was out, Eunice examined every object in Lowfield Hall at her leisure. The house had been dirty by her standards. It brought her intense pleasure to subject it to a spring-cleaning. Oh, the lovely carpets, the hangings, the cushions, the rosewood and walnut and oak, the glass and silver and china! But best of all was the kitchen with pine walls and cupboards, a double steel sink, a washing machine, a dryer, a dishwasher. It wasn't enough for her to dust the porcelain in the drawing room. It must be washed.

'You really need not do that, Miss Parchman.'

'I like doing it,' said Eunice.

Fear of breakages rather than altruism had prompted Jacqueline to protest. But Eunice never broke anything, nor

45

did she fail to replace anything to the exact spot from where she had taken it. Her visual memory imprinted neat permanent photographs in some department of her brain.

The only things in Lowfield Hall which didn't interest her and which she didn't handle or study were the contents of the morning-room desk, the books, the letters from George in Jacqueline's dressing table. Those things and, at this stage, the two shotguns.

Her employers were overwhelmed.

'She's perfect.' said Jacqueline who, parcelling up George's shirts for the laundry, had had them taken out of her hands by Eunice and laundered exquisitely between defrosting the fridge and changing the bed linen. 'D'you know what she said, darling? She just looked at me in that meek way she has and said, "Give me those. I like a bit of ironing." '

Meek? Eunice Parchman?

'She's certainly very efficient,' said George. 'And I like to see you looking so happy and relaxed.'

'Well, I don't have a thing to do. Apart from her putting the green sheets on our bed once and simply ignoring a note I left her, I haven't had a fault to find. It seems absurd calling those things faults after old Eva and that dreadful Ingrid.'

'How does she get on with Eva?'

'Ignores her, I think. I wish I had the nerve. D'you know, Miss Parchman can sew too. I was trying to turn up the hem of my green skirt, and she took it and did it perfectly.'

'We've been very lucky,' said George.

So the month of May passed. The spring flowers died away and the trees sprang into leaf. Pheasants came into the fields to eat the green corn, and the nightingale sang in the orchard. But not for Eunice. Hares, alert and quivering, cropped under the hedges, and the moon rose slowly behind the Greeving Hills, red and strange like another sun. But not for Eunice. She drew the curtains, put on the lamps and then the television. Her evenings were hers to do as she liked. This was what she liked. She knitted. But gradually, as the serial or the sporting event or the cops and robbers film began to grip her, the knitting fell into her lap and she leant forwards, enthralled by an innocent childlike excitement.

She was happy. If she had been capable of analysing her thoughts and feelings and of questioning her motives she would have said that this vicarious living was better than any life she had known. But had she been capable of that it is unlikely she would have been content with so specious a way of spending her leisure. Her addiction gives rise to a question. Wouldn't some social service have immensely benefited society – and saved the lives of the Coverdales – had it recognized Eunice Parchman's harmless craving? Give her a room, a pension and a television set and leave her to worship and to stare for the rest of her life? No social service came into contact with her until it was far too late. No psychiatrist had ever seen her. Such a one would only have discovered the root cause of her neurosis if she had allowed him to discover her illiteracy. And she had been expert at concealing it since the time when she might have been expected to overcome it. Her father, who could read perfectly well, who in his youth had read the Bible from beginning to end, was her principal ally in helping her hide her deficiency. He who should have encouraged her to learn instead conspired with her in the far more irksome complexities not learning entailed.

When a neighbour, dropping in with a newspaper, had handed it to Eunice, 'I'll have that,' he had been used to say, looking at the small print, 'don't strain her young eyes.' It came to be accepted in her narrow circle that Eunice had poor sight, this solution generally being the one seized upon by the uneducated literate to account for illiteracy.

'Can't read it? You mean you can't *see*?'

When she was a child she had never wanted to read. As she grew older she wanted to learn, but who could teach her? Acquiring a teacher, or even trying to acquire one, would mean other people finding out. She had begun to shun other people, all of whom seemed to her bent on ferreting out her secret. After a time this shunning, this isolating herself, became automatic, though the root cause of her misanthropy was half-forgotten.

Things could not hurt her – the furniture, the ornaments, the television – she embraced them, they aroused in her the nearest she ever got to warm emotion, while to the Coverdales she gave the cold shoulder. Not that they received more of her stoniness than anyone else had done; she behaved to them as she had always behaved to everyone.

George was the first to notice it. Of all the Coverdales he was by far the most sensitive, and therefore the first to see a flaw in all this excellence.

Chapter 6

They sat in church on Sunday morning and Mr Archer began to preach his sermon. For his text he took: 'Well done, thou good and faithful servant. Thou hast been faithful over a few things; I will make thee ruler over many things.' Jacqueline smiled at George and touched his arm, and he smiled back, well satisfied.

On the following day he remembered those exchanged smiles and thought he had been fatuous, perhaps over-complacent.

'Paula's gone into hospital,' Jacqueline said when George came home. 'It's really rather awful the way they fix a day for your baby to be born these days. Just take you in and give you an injection and Hey presto!'

'Instant infants,' said George. 'Has Brian phoned?'

'Not since two.'

'I'll just give him a ring.'

They would be dining, as they often did when alone, in the morning room. Eunice came in to lay the table. George dialled but there was no reply. A second after he put the phone down it rang. After answering Paula's husband in monosyllables and a final 'Call me back soon,' he walked over to Jacqueline and took her hand.

'There's some complication. They haven't decided yet, but she's very exhausted and it'll probably mean an emergency Caesarean.'

'Darling, I'm so sorry, what a worry!' She didn't tell him

not to worry, and he was glad of it. 'Why don't you phone Dr Crutchley? He might reassure you.'

'I'll do that.'

Eunice left the room. George appreciated her tactful silence. He phoned the doctor who said he couldn't comment on a case he knew nothing about, and reassured George only to the extent of telling him that, generally speaking, women didn't die in childbirth any more.

They ate their dinner. That is, Giles ate his dinner, Jacqueline picked at hers, and George left his almost untouched. Giles made one small concession to the seriousness of the occasion and the anxiety of the others. He stopped reading and stared instead into space. Afterwards, when the suspense was over, Jacqueline said laughingly to her husband that such a gesture from Giles was comparable to a pep talk and a bottle of brandy from anyone else.

The suspense didn't last long. Brian called back twice, and half an hour after that was on the line to say a seven-pound boy had been delivered by Caesarean operation and Paula was well.

Eunice was clearing the table. She must have heard it all, George's 'Thank God!', Jacqueline's 'That's wonderful, darling. I'm so happy for you,' Giles's 'Good,' before he took himself off upstairs. She must have heard relief and seen delight. Without the slightest reaction, she left the room and closed the door.

Jacqueline put her arms round George and held him. He didn't think about Eunice then. It was only as he was going to bed and heard faintly above him the hum of her television that he began to think her behaviour strangely cold. Not once had she expressed her concern during the anxious time, nor her satisfaction for him when the danger was past. Consciously he hadn't waited for her to do so. At the time he hadn't expected a 'I'm so glad to hear your daughter's all right, sir', but now he wondered at the omission. It troubled him.

Lack of care for a fellow woman, lack of concern for the people in whose home one lived, were unnatural in any woman. Well done, thou good and faithful servant... But that had not been well done.

Not for the world would George have spoken of his unease to Jacqueline who was so happy and contented with her employee. Besides, he wouldn't have wanted a loquacious servant, making the family's affairs her affairs and being familiar. He resolved to banish it from his mind.

And this he did quite successfully until the christening of the new baby which took place a month later.

Patrick had been christened at Greeving; Mr Archer was a friend of the Coverdales, and a country christening in summer is pleasanter than one in town. Paula and Brian and their two children arrived at Lowfield Hall on a Saturday at the end of June and stayed till the Sunday. They had quite a large party on the Saturday afternoon. Brian's parents and his sister were there, as well as the Roystons, the Jameson-Kerrs, an aunt of Jacqueline's from Bury and some cousins of George from Newmarket. And the arrangements for eating and drinking, carried out by Eunice under Jacqueline's directions, were perfect. The house had never looked so nice, the champagne glasses so well polished. Jacqueline didn't know they possessed so many white linen table napkins, had never seen them all together before and all so freshly starched. In the past she had sometimes been reduced to using paper ones.

Before they left for the church Melinda came into the drawing room to show Eunice the baby. He was to be called Giles, and Giles Mont, aghast at the idea now, had been roped in to be godfather before he realized what was happening. She carried him in in the long embroidered christening robe that she herself, her brother and sister, and indeed George himself, had once worn. He was a fine-looking baby, large and red and lusty. On the table, beside the cake, was the Coverdales' christening book, a volume of listed names of those who had worn the robe, when and where they had been baptized and so on. It was open, ready for this latest entry.

'Isn't he *sweet,* Miss Parchman?'

Eunice stood chill and stiff. George felt a coldness come from her as if the sun had gone in. She didn't smile or bend over the baby or make as if to touch his coverings. She looked at him. It wasn't a look of enthusiasm such as George had seen her give to the silver spoons when she laid them out on the saucers. Having looked at him, she said:

'I must get on. I've things to see to.'

Not one word did he or Jacqueline receive from her during the course of the afternoon when she was in and out with trays as to the attractiveness of the child, their luck in having such a fine day, or the happiness of the young parents. Cold, he thought, unnaturally cold. Or was she just painfully shy?

Eunice was not shy. Nor had she turned from the baby because she was afraid of the book. Not directly. She was simply uninterested in the baby. But it would be true to say that she was uninterested in babies because there are books in the world.

The printed word was horrible to her, a personal threat to her. Keep away from it, avoid it, and from all those who will show it to her. The habit of shunning it was ingrained in her; it was no longer conscious. All the springs of warmth and outgoing affection and human enthusiasm had been dried up long ago by it. Isolating herself was natural now, and she was not aware that it had begun by isolating herself from print and books and handwriting.

Illiteracy had dried up her sympathy and atrophied her imagination. That, along with what psychologists call *affect,* the ability to care about the feelings of others, had no place in her make-up.

General Gordon, in attempting to raise the morale of the

besieged inhabitants of Khartoum, told them that when God was handing out fear to the people of the world, at last he came to him. But by that time God had no more fear to give, so Gordon was created without fear. This elegant parable may be paraphrased for Eunice. When God came to her, he had no more imagination or affect to give.

The Coverdales were interferers. They interfered with the best intentions, those of making other people happy. If it were not such an awful thing to say of anyone (to quote one of Giles Mont's favourite authors) one could say that they meant well. They were afraid of being selfish, for they had never understood what Giles knew instinctively, that selfishness is not living as one wishes to live, it is asking others to live as one wishes to live.

'I'm worried about old Parchment Face,' said Melinda. 'Don't you think she has a terrible life?'

'I don't know,' said Giles. Melinda was paying one of her rare visits to his room, sitting in fact on his bed, and this both made him happy and threw him into a panic. 'I haven't noticed.'

'Oh, you – you never notice anything. But I can tell you she does. She's never once been out, not all the time she's been here. All she does is watch television. Listen, it's on now.' She paused dramatically and turned her eyes up to the ceiling. Giles went on with what he had been doing when she first came in, pinning things up on the cork tiles with which he had covered half one of the walls. 'She must be terribly lonely,' said Melinda. 'She must miss her friends.' She grabbed Giles by the arm and swung him round. 'Don't you *care*?'

Her touch gave him a shock and he blushed. 'Leave her alone. She's all right.'

'She's not. She can't be.'

'Some people like being alone.' He looked vaguely round his room, at the heap of orange clothes, the muddle of books and dictionaries, the stacks of half-finished essays on subjects not in the Magnus Wythen curriculum. He loved it. It was better than anywhere else except possibly the London Library where he had once been taken by a scholarly relative. But they won't let you rent a room in the London Library, or Giles would have been at the top of their housing list. 'I like being alone,' he said.

'If that's a hint to me to go...'

'No, no, it isn't,' he said hastily, and resolving to declare himself, began in a hoarse thrilling voice, 'Melinda...'

'What? Where did you get that awful poster? Is she supposed to have a green face?'

Giles sighed. The moment had passed. 'Read my Quote of the Month.'

It was written in green ink on a piece of paper pinned to the cork wall. Melinda read it aloud. ' "Why should the generations overlap one another at all? Why cannot we be buried as eggs in neat little cells with ten or twenty thousand pounds each wrapped round us in Bank of England notes, and wake up, as the sphex wasp does, to find that its papa and mamma have not only left ample provision at its elbow but have been eaten by sparrows some weeks before?" '

'Good, isn't it? Samuel Butler.'

'You can't have that on the wall, Step. If Daddy or Jackie saw it, it'd absolutely freak them out. Anyway, I thought you were supposed to be doing classics.'

'I may not do anything,' said Giles. 'I may go to India. I don't suppose,' greatly daring, 'you'd want to come too?'

Melinda made a face. 'I bet you don't go. You *know* you won't. You're just trying to get off a subject that might involve you. I was going to ask you to come down with me and *confront* Daddy and make him do something about her. But I bet you'll say you won't.'

Giles pushed his fingers through his hair. He would have liked to please her. She was the only person in the world he cared much about pleasing. But there were limits. Not even for her would he defy his principles and flout his nature. 'No,' he said, and gloomily, almost sorrowfully, contorting his face in a kind of hopelessness, 'no, I won't do that.'

'Mad,' said Melinda and bounced out.

Her father and Jacqueline were in the garden, in the midsummer dusk, surveying what Jacqueline had done that day. There was a heavy sweet scent from the first flowers on the tobacco plants.

'I've been thinking, my darlings. We ought to do something about poor old Parchment Face, take her out, give her an interest.'

Her stepmother gave her a cool smile. In some respects Jacqueline could fill the wasp role her son had meted out to her. 'Not everyone is such an extrovert as you, you know.'

'And I think we've had enough of that Parchment Face business, Melinda,' said George. 'You're no longer the naughtiest girl in the sixth.'

'Now you're evading the issue.'

'No, we're not. Jackie and I have been discussing that very thing. We're quite aware *Miss* Parchman hasn't been out, but she may not know where to go, and it's difficult without a car.'

'Then lend her a car! We've got two.'

'That's what we're going to do. The chances are she's too shy to ask. I see her as a very shy woman.'

'Repressed by a ruling class,' said Melinda.

It was Jacqueline who made the offer.

'I can't drive,' said Eunice. She didn't mind saying this. There were only two things she minded admitting she couldn't do. Hardly anyone in her circle had been able to drive, and in Rainbow Street it had been looked on as a rather bizarre accomplishment for a woman. 'I never learnt.'

'What a pity! I was going to say you could borrow my car. I really don't know how you'll get around without transport.'

'I can go on the bus.' Eunice vaguely supposed a red double-decker trundled around the lanes with the frequency of the 88 in Tooting.

'That's just what you can't do. The nearest bus stop's two miles away, and there are only three buses a day.'

Just as George had detected a flaw in his housekeeper, so now Eunice sensed a small cloud threatening her peaceful life. This was the first time any Coverdale had shown signs of wanting to change it. She waited uneasily for the next move, and she didn't have to wait long.

Progenitor of Coverdales, George was the arch-interferer of them all. Employees were hauled into his office at TBC and advised about their marriages, their mortgages and the higher education of their children. Meadows, Higgs and Carter matrons were accustomed to his entering their cottages and being told to get the dry-rot people in, or why not grow a few vegetables on that piece of ground? Ever such a nice man was Mr Coverdale, but you don't want to take no notice of what he says. Different in my gran's time. The squire was the squire then, but them old days are gone, thank God. George went on interfering – for the good of others.

He bearded the lion in its den. The lion looked very tame and was occupied in womanly fashion, ironing one of his dress shirts.

'Yes, sir?' Her tabby-cat hair was neatly combed, and she wore a blue and white checked cotton dress.

All his life George had been looked after by women, but none of them had ever attempted the formidable task of washing, starching and ironing a 'boiled' shirt. George, if he ever thought about it at all, supposed that there was a special mystique attached to these operations, and that they could only be performed in a laundry by a clever machine. He smiled approvingly.

'Ah, I can see I'm interrupting an expert at a very skilled task. You're making a fine job of that, Miss Parchman.'

'I like ironing,' said Eunice.

'I'm glad to hear it, but I don't suppose you like being confined at Lowfield Hall all the time, do you? That's what I've come to talk about. My wife tells me you've never found time in your busy life to learn to drive a car. Am I right?'

'Yes,' said Eunice.

'I see. Well, we shall have to remedy that. What would you say to driving lessons? I shall be happy to foot the bill. We're doing well by you and we'd like to do something for you in return.'

'I couldn't learn to drive,' said Eunice who had been thinking hard. The favourite excuse came out. 'My sight wouldn't be up to it.'

'You don't wear glasses.'

'I should do. I'm waiting for my new pair.'

In-depth questioning elicited that Eunice should have glasses, had been in need of new ones when she came to Greeving, had 'let it slide', couldn't, even with glasses, read a number plate or a road sign. She must have her eyes tested forthwith, said George; he would see to it himself and drive her into Stantwich.

'I feel rather ashamed of myself,' he said to Jacqueline. 'All the time the poor woman was as blind as a bat. I don't mind telling you now we know the reason for it, but I was beginning to find that reserve of hers quite off-putting.'

Alarm showed in her eyes. 'Oh, George, you mustn't say that! Having her has made such a difference to my life.'

'I'm not saying a thing, darling. I quite understand she's very short-sighted and was much too diffident to say so.'

'The working classes are absurd about things like that,' said Jacqueline, who would have suffered agonies struggling with contact lenses, would have bumped into walls rather than wear glasses. They both felt immensely satisfied with George's discovery, and it occurred to neither of them that a purblind woman could hardly have cleaned the windows to a diamond brilliance or watched the television for three hours every evening.

Chapter 7

At forty-seven, Eunice had better sight than Giles Mont at seventeen. Sitting beside George in the car, she wondered what to do if he insisted on coming into the optician's with her. She was unable to concoct any excuse to avoid this happening, and her experience was inadequate to teach her that middle-aged conservative landowners do not generally accompany their middle-aged female servants into what is virtually a doctor's surgery. A sullen puzzled resentment simmered within her. The last man who sought to make her life insupportable got a pillow over his face for his pains.

A slight fillip came to her spirits at the sight, at last, of shops, those familiar and wonderful treasure houses that had seemed left behind for ever. They got an even greater lift when George showed no sign of accompanying her into the optician's. He left her with a promise to be back in half an hour and the instruction to have any bill sent to him.

Once the car had gone, Eunice walked round the corner where she had noticed a confectioner's. She bought two Kit-Kats, a Mars bar and a bag of marshmallows, and then she went into a teashop. There she had a cup of tea, a currant bun and a chocolate eclair, which made a nice change from cassoulets and vine leaves and all those made-up dishes she got at Lowfield Hall. The picture of respectability was Eunice on that Saturday morning, sitting upright at her table in her navy blue crimplene suit, nylon stockings, Annie Cole's mother's court shoes, an 'invisible' net on her hair.

No one would have supposed her mind was racing on lines of deception – deception that comes so easily to those who can read and write and have IQs of 120. But at last a plan was formed. She crossed the road to Boots and bought two pairs of sunglasses, not dark ones but faintly tinted, one pair with a crystal blue frame, the other of mock tortoise-shell. Into her handbag with them, not to be produced for a week.

The Coverdales seemed surprised they would be ready so quickly. She was taken to Stantwich the second time by Jacqueline, who luckily didn't go with her into the optician's because of the impossibility of parking on a double yellow line. It was bad enough having to pay the fines incurred by Giles. Eunice bought more chocolate and consumed more cake. She showed the glasses to Jacqueline and went so far as to put the crystal blue pair on. In them she felt a fool. Must she wear them all the time now, she who could see the feathers on a sparrow's wing in the orchard a hundred feet away? And would they expect her to *read*?

Nobody really lives in the present. But Eunice did so more than most people. For her five minutes' delay in dinner now was more important than a great sorrow ten years gone, and to the future she had never given much thought. But now, with the glasses in her possession, occasionally even on her nose, she became very aware of the printed word which surrounded her and to which, at some future time, she might be expected to react.

Lowfield Hall was full of books. It seemed to Eunice that there were as many books here as in Tooting Public Library where once, and once only, she had been to return an overdue novel of Mrs Samson's. She saw them as small flattish boxes, packed with mystery and threat. One entire wall of the morning room was filled with bookshelves; in the drawing room great glass-fronted bookcases stood on either side of the fireplace and more shelves filled the twin alcoves. There were books on bedside tables, magazines and newspapers in racks. And they read books all the time. It seemed to her that they must read to provoke her, for no one, not even schoolteachers, could read that much for pleasure. Giles was never without a book in his hand. He even brought his reading matter into her kitchen and sat absorbed in it, his elbows on the table. Jacqueline read every new novel of note, and she and George re-read their way through Victorian novels, their closeness emphasized by their often reading some work of Dickens or Thackeray or George Eliot at the same time, so as later to discuss a character or a scene together. Incongruously, it was the student of English literature who read the least, but even so Melinda was often to be found in the garden or lying on the morning-room floor with one of Mr Sweet's grammars before her. This was not from inclination but because of a menace from her tutor – 'If we're going to make the grade we shall have to come to grips with those Anglo-Saxon pronouns before next term, shan't we?' But how was Eunice to know that?

She had been happy, but the glasses had destroyed her happiness. She had been content with the house and the lovely things in the house, and the Coverdales had hardly existed for her, so little notice had she taken of them. Now she could hardly wait for them to go away on that summer holiday they were always talking about and planning.

But before they went, and they were not going until the beginning of August, before their departure set her free to expand, to explore, and to meet Joan Smith, three unpleasant things happened.

The first was nothing in itself. It was what it led up to that bothered Eunice. She dropped one of Geoff Baalham's eggs on the kitchen floor. Jacqueline, who was there, said only, 'Oh, dear, what a mess!' and Eunice had cleaned it up in a flash. But on the following morning she went up to turn out Giles's bedroom, always a formidable task, and for the first time she allowed herself to look at his cork wall. Why? She could hardly have answered that herself, but perhaps it was because she was now equipped to read, made vulnerable, as it were, to reading, and because she had now become aware of the oppressive number of books in the house. There was a message on the wall beside that nasty poster. 'Why' it began. She could read that word without much difficulty when it was printed. 'One' she could also read and 'eggs'. Giles evidently meant it for her and was reproaching her for breaking that egg. She didn't care for his reproaches, but suppose he broke his silence – he never spoke to her – to ask her why. Why hadn't she obeyed his 'why' message? He might tell his stepfather, and Eunice was on tenterhooks whenever George looked at her unbespectacled face.

At last the message was taken down, but only to be replaced by another. Eunice was almost paralysed by it, and for a week she did no more in Giles's room than pull up the bedclothes and open the window. She was as frightened of those pieces of paper as another woman would have been had Giles kept a snake in his room.

But not so frightened as she was of Jacqueline's note, the third unpleasant incident. This was left on the kitchen table one morning while Eunice was at the top of the house making her own bed. When she came downstairs, Jacqueline had driven off to London to see Paula, to have her hair cut and to buy clothes for her holiday.

Jacqueline had left notes for her before, and had wondered why the otherwise obedient Miss Parchman never obeyed the behests in them. All, however, was explained by her poor sight. But now Eunice had her glasses. Not that she was wearing them. They were upstairs, stuffed into the bottom of her knitting bag. She stared at the note, which meant as much to her as a note in Greek would have meant to Jacqueline – precisely as much, for Jacqueline could recognize an alpha, an omega and a pi just as Eunice knew some capital letters and the odd monosyllabic word. But connecting those words, deciphering longer ones, making anything of it, that was beyond her. In London she would have had Annie Cole to help her. Here she had no one but Giles, who wandered through the kitchen to cadge a lift to Stantwich, to moon about the shops and spend the afternoon in a dark cinema. He didn't so much as glance at her, and she would rather anything than ask help from him.

It wasn't one of Eva Baalham's days. Could she lose the note? Inventiveness was not among her gifts. It had taken all her puny powers to convince George that the optician's bill hadn't come because she had already paid it, liked to be independent, didn't want to be 'beholden'.

And then Melinda came in.

Eunice had forgotten she was in the house, she couldn't get used to these bits of kids starting their summer holidays in June. Melinda danced in at midday, pretty healthy buxom Melinda in too-tight jeans and a Mickey Mouse tee-shirt, yellow hair in Dutch-girl pigtails, her feet bare. The sun was shining, a wind was blowing, the whole kitchen was radiated with fluttering dancing sunbeams, and Melinda was off to the seaside with two boys and another girl in an orange and purple painted van. She picked up the note and read it aloud. 'What's this? "Please would you be awfully kind and if you have the time press my yellow silk, the one with the pleated skirt. I want to wear it tonight. It's in my wardrobe somewhere up on the right. Thank you so much, J.C." It must be for you, Miss Parchman. D'you think you could do my red skirt at the same time? *Would* you?'

'Oh, yes, it's no trouble,' said the much-relieved Eunice with quite a broad smile for her.

'You are *sweet*,' said Melinda.

August came in with a heatwave, and Mr Meadows, the

farmer whose land adjoined George's, began cutting his wheat. The new combine harvester dropped bales of straw shaped like slices of Swiss roll. Melinda picked fruit, along with the village women, in the cherry orchards, Giles put up a new Quote of the Month, again from Samuel Butler, Jacqueline weeded the garden and found a thorn-apple, poisonous but beautiful and bearing a single white trumpet flower among the zinnias. And at last it was time to go away, 7 August.

'I won't forget to send you a card,' said Melinda, recalling as she did from time to time that it was her duty to cheer old Parchment Face up.

'You'll find any numbers and addresses you may want in the directory by the phone.' This from Jacqueline, while George said, 'You can always send us a telegram in case of emergency.'

Useless, all of it, had they but known.

Eunice saw them off from the front door, wearing the crystal blue glasses to allay admonition. A soft haze lay over Greeving at this early hour, a haze thickened by smoke, for Mr Meadows was burning the stubble off his fields. Eunice didn't linger to appreciate the great purple dahlias, drenched with dew, or listen to the cuckoo's last calls before his departure. She went quickly indoors to possess what she had looked forward to.

Her purpose didn't include neglecting the house, and she went through her usual Friday routine, but with certain additional tasks. She stripped the beds, threw away the flower arrangements – more or less dead, anyway, nasty messy things, dropping petals everywhere – and hid, as best she could, every book, magazine and newspaper. She would have liked to cover the bookcases with sheets, but only madness goes that far, and Eunice was not mad.

Then she cooked herself a dinner. The Coverdales would have called it lunch because it was eaten at one o'clock. They were not to know how dreadfully their housekeeper had missed a good solid hot meal eaten in the middle of the day. Eunice fried (fried, not grilled) a big steak from the deep-freeze, fried potatoes too, while the runner beans, the carrots and the parsnips were boiling. Apple pudding and custard to follow, biscuits and cheese and strong black tea. She washed the dishes, dried them and put them away. It was a relief not to be obliged to use that dishwasher. She never had liked the idea of dirty plates with gravy or crumbs all over them hanging about in there all day, even though the door was shut and you couldn't see them.

Mrs Sampson used to say that a woman's work is never done. Not even the most house-proud could have found more work to be done in Lowfield Hall that day. Tomorrow she would think about taking down the morning-room curtains, but not today, not now. Now for a thoroughgoing indulgence in, an orgy of, television.

7 August was to be recorded as the hottest day of the year. The temperature rose to seventy-eight, eighty, until by half past two it touched eighty-five. In Greeving, jam-making housewives left their kitchens and took the sun on back doorsteps; the weir on the River Beal became a swimming pool for little Higgses and Baalhams; farm dogs hung out their tongues; Mrs Cairne forgot discretion and lay on her front lawn in a bikini; Joan Smith propped her shop door open with a box of dog biscuits and fanned herself with a fly swat. But Eunice went upstairs, drew her curtains, and settled down in deep contentment with her knitting in front of the screen. All she needed to make her happiness perfect was a bar of chocolate, but she had long ago eaten up all those she had bought in Stantwich.

Sport first. People swimming and people racing round stadiums. Then a serial about much the same sort of characters as those Eunice had known in Rainbow Street, a children's programme, the news, the weather forecast. She never cared much for the news, and anyone could see and feel what the weather was and was going to be. She went downstairs and fetched herself jam sandwiches and a block of chocolate ice-cream. At eight o'clock her favourite programme of the entire week was due to begin, a series about policemen in Los Angeles. It is hard to say why Eunice loved it so much. Certainly she confounded those analysts of escape channels who say that an audience must identify. Eunice couldn't identify with the young police lieutenant or his twenty-year-old blonde girl friend or with the gangsters, tycoons, film stars, call girls, gamblers and drunks who abounded in each adventure. Perhaps it was the clipped harsh repartee she liked, the inevitable car chase and the indispensable shooting. It had irked her exceedingly to miss an episode as she had often done in the past, the Coverdales seeming deliberately to single out Friday as their entertaining night.

There was no one to disturb her this time. She laid down her knitting the better to concentrate. It was going to be a good story tonight, she could tell that from the opening sequence, a corpse in the first two minutes and a car chase in the first five. The gunman's car crashed, half-mounting a lamp-post. The car door opened, the gunman leapt out and across the street, firing his gun, dodging a policeman's bullets into the shelter of a porch, pulling a frightened girl in front of him as his shield, again taking aim... Suddenly the sound faded and the picture began to dwindle, to shrink, as it was sucked into a spot in the centre of the screen like black water draining into a hole. The spot shone like a star, a tiny point of light that burned brightly and went out.

Eunice switched it off, switched it on again. Nothing happened. She moved knobs on the front of it and even those knobs on the back they said you should never touch. Nothing happened. She opened the plug and checked that the wires were all where they ought to be. She took out the fuse and replaced it with one from her bed lamp.

66

The screen remained blank, or, rather, had become merely a mirror, reflecting her own dismayed face and the hot red sunset burning through a chink between the closed curtains.

Chapter 8

It never occurred to her to use the colour set in the morning room. She knew it was usable, but it was *theirs*. A curious feature of Eunice Parchman's character was that, although she did not stop at murder or blackmail, she never in her life stole anything or even borrowed anything without its owner's consent. Objects, like spheres of life, were appointed, predestined, to certain people. Eunice no more cared to see the order of things disturbed than George did.

For a while she hoped that the set would right itself, start up as spontaneously as it had failed. But each time she switched it on it remained blank and silent. Of course she knew that when things went wrong you sent for the man to put them right. In Tooting you went round to the ironmonger's or the electric people. But here? With only a phone and an indecipherable list of names and numbers, a useless incomprehensible directory?

Saturday, Sunday, Monday. The milkman called and Geoff Baalham brought the eggs. Ask them and have them tell her to look such and such a number up in the phone book? She was cruelly bored and frustrated. There were no neighbours with whom to pass the time of day, no busy street to watch, no buses or teashops. She took down the curtains, washed and ironed them, washed paintwork, shampooed the carpets, anything to pass the slow, heavy, lumbering time.

It was Eva Baalham, arriving on Wednesday, who discovered what had happened, simply as a result of asking Eunice if she had watched the big fight on the previous evening. And Eva only asked that for something to say, talking to Miss Parchman being a sticky business at the best of times.

'Broke down?' said Eva. 'I reckon you'll have to have that seen to then. My cousin Meadows that keeps the electric shop in Gosbury, he'd do that for you. I tell you what, I'll leave doing the old bits of silver till Friday and give him a ring.'

Along dialogue ensued with someone called Rodge in which Eva enquired after Doris and Mum and 'the boy' and 'the girl' (young married people, these last, with children of their own) and finally got a promise of assistance.

'He says he'll pop in when he knocks off.'

'Hope he doesn't have to take it away,' said Eunice.

'Never know with they old sets, do you? You'll have to have a look at the paper instead.'

Literacy is in our veins like blood. It enters every other phrase. It is next to impossible to hold a real conversation, as against an interchange of instructions and acquiescences, in which reference to the printed word is not made or in which the implications of something read do not occur.

Rodge Meadows came and he did have to take the set away.

'Could be a couple of days, could be a week. Give me a ring if you don't hear nothing from Auntie Eva. I'm in the book.'

Two days later, in the solitude and silence and boredom of Lowfield Hall, a compulsion came over Eunice. Without any idea of where to go or why she was going, she found herself changing the blue and white check dress for the crimplene suit, and then making her first unescorted assay into the outside world. She closed all the windows, bolted the front door, locked the door of the gun room, and started off down the drive. It was 14 August. If the television set hadn't broken down she would never have gone. Sooner or later one of her own urges or the efforts of the Coverdales would have got her out of that house but she would have gone in the evening or on a Sunday afternoon when Greeving Post Office and Village Store, Prop. N. Smith, would have been closed. If, if, if... If she had been able to read, the television might still have held charms for her, but she would have looked the engineer's number up in the phone book on Saturday morning, and by Tuesday or Wednesday she would have had that set back. On Saturday the 15th, Rodge did, in fact, return it, but by then it was too late and the damage was done.

She didn't know where she was going. Even then, it was touch and go whether she went to Creeving at all, for she took the first turn off the lane, and two miles and three-quarters of an hour later she was in Cocklefield St Jude. Not much more than a hamlet is Cocklefield St Jude, with an enormous church but no shop. Eunice came to a crossroads. The signpost was useless to her but she wasn't afraid of getting lost. God tempers the wind to the shorn lamb, and as compensation perhaps for her singular misfortune she had been endowed with a sense of direction that was almost as good as an animal's. Accordingly, she took the narrowest exit from the cross which led her down a sequestered defile, a lane no more than eight feet wide and overhung with the dark late-summer foliage of ash and oak, and where one car could not pass another without drawing deep into the hedge.

Eunice had never been in such a place in her life. A cow with a face like a great white ghost stuck its head over the hedge and lowed at her. In a sunny patch, where there was a gap in the trees, a cock pheasant with clattering feathers lolloped across in front of her, all gilded chestnut and fiery green. She marched on, head up, alarmed but resolute, knowing she was going the right way.

And so, at last, to Greeving and into the heart of the village itself, for the lane came out opposite the Blue Boar. She turned right, and having passed the terrace of cottages inhabited by various Higgses and Newsteads and Carters, the small Georgian mansion of Mrs Cairne and the discreet, soberly decorated neon-less petrol station kept by Jim Meadows, she found herself on the triangle of turf outside the village store.

The shop was double-fronted, being a conversion of the ground floor of a largish, very old cottage, whose front gable was half-timbered and whose roof was badly in need of rethatching. Behind it was a garden which sloped down to the banks of the Beal that, at this point, curved out of the meadows to run under Greeving Bridge. Greeving Village Store is now efficiently run by Mr and Mrs Mann, but at that time the two large windows held a dusty display of cereal packets, canned fruit, and baskets of not very fresh-looking tomatoes and cabbages. Eunice approached one of these windows and looked inside. The shop was empty. It was often empty, for the Smiths charged high prices while necessarily stocking only a small selection of goods. Greeving residents with cars preferred the supermarkets of Stantwich and Nunchester, availing themselves only of the post office facilities of their village store.

Eunice went in. On the left the shop was arranged for self-service with wire baskets provided. On the right was a typical sub-post-office counter and grille with, beside it, a display of sweets and cigarettes. At one time there had been a bell which rang each time the door was opened, but this had gone wrong and the Smiths had never had it mended. Therefore, no one heard her enter. Eunice examined the shelves with interest, noting the presence of various commodities she well knew from shopping expeditions in South London. But she couldn't read? Yet who does *read* the name of a product or its manufacturer's name on a packet or tin? One goes by the colour and the shape

71

and the picture as much as if one is a professor of etymology as an illiterate.

It was a month since she had tasted a sweet. Now she thought the most desirable thing in the world would be to have a box of chocolates. So she walked up to the counter on the left of the grille and, having waited in vain for a few seconds, she coughed. Her cough resulted in a door at the back of the shop opening and in the appearance of a woman some few years older than herself.

Joan Smith was at this time fifty, thin as a starved bird, with matchstick bones and chicken skin. Her hair was the same colour as Jacqueline Coverdale's, each aiming, of course, at attaining Melinda's natural fine gold by artificial means. Jacqueline was more successful because she had more money to spend. Joan Smith's coiffure, wiry, stiff, glittering, had the look of one of the yellow metal pot-scourers displayed for sale on her shelves. Her face was haphazardly painted, her hands red, rough and untended. In her shrill voice, cockney overlaid with refinement, not unlike Annie Cole's she asked Eunice what she could do for her.

For the first time the two women looked at each other, small blue eyes meeting sharp grey ones.

'Pound box of Black Magic, please,' said Eunice.

How many thousands of pairs of people, brought together into a partnership for passion, for pain, for profit or for disaster, have commenced their relationship with words as mundane as these?

Joan produced the chocolates. She always had a sprightly manner, coy, girlish, arch. Impossible for her simply to hand an object to anyone and take the money. First must come elaborate flourishes, a smile, a little hop that almost lifted her feet out of her Minnie Mouse shoes, her head roguishly on one side. Even towards her religion, she kept up a familiar jolly attitude. The Lord was her friend, brutal to the unregenerate, but matey and intimate with the chosen, the kind of pal you might take to the pictures and have a bit of a giggle with afterwards over a nice cuppa.

'Eighty-five pee,' said Joan, 'if you *please.*' She rang it up on the till, eyeing Eunice with a little whimsical smile. 'And how are they all enjoying their holiday, or haven't you heard?'

Eunice was amazed. She didn't know, and was never really to know, that very little can be kept secret in an English village. Not only did everyone in Greeving know where the Coverdales had gone when they had gone, when they were coming back and roughly what their trip cost, but they were already aware that she herself had paid her first visit to the village that afternoon. Nellie Higgs and Jim Meadows had spotted her, the grapevine was at work, and her appearance and the motive for her walk would be discussed and speculated about in the Blue Boar that night. But to Eunice that Joan Smith should recognize her and know where she worked was little short of magical divination. It awoke in her a kind of wondering admiration. It laid the foundation of her dependence on Joan and her belief, generally speaking, in the rightness of everything Joan said.

But all she said then was, 'I haven't heard.'

'Well, early days yet. Lovely to get away for three weeks, isn't it? Chance'd be a fine thing. Ever such a nice family, aren't they? Mr Coverdale is what I call a real gentleman of the old school, and she's a real lady. Never think she was forty-eight, would you?' Thus Joan added six years to poor Jacqueline's age from no motive but pure malice. In fact, she heartily disliked the Coverdales because they never patronized her shop, and George had been known to criticize the running of the post office. But she had no intention of admitting these feelings to Eunice until she saw how the land lay. 'You're lucky to work for them, but they're lucky to have you, from all I've heard.'

'I don't know,' said Eunice.

'Oh, you're being modest, I can see that. A little bird told me the Hall'd never looked so spick and span. Makes a change, I dare say, after old Eva giving it a lick and a promise all these years. Don't you get a bit lonesome, though?'

'I've got the TV,' said Eunice, beginning to expand, 'and there's always a job wants doing.'

'You're right. I know I'm run off my feet with this place, it's all go. Not a churchgoer, are you? No, I'd have spotted you if you'd been to St Mary's with the family.'

'I'm not religious. Never seemed to have the time.'

'Ah, you don't know what you miss,' said proselytizing Joan, wagging a forefinger. 'But it's never too late, remember. The patience of the Lord is infinite and the bridegroom is ever ready to welcome you to his feast. Lovely weather he's sending us, isn't it, especially for those as don't have to sweat their guts out slaving for others.'

'I'll be getting back now,' said Eunice.

'Pity Norm's got the van or I could run you back.' Joan came to the door with Eunice and turned the notice to Closed. 'Got your chocs? That's right. Now, don't forget, if ever you're at a loose end, I'm always here. Don't be afraid of putting me out. I've always got a cup of tea and a cheery word for a friend.'

'I won't,' said Eunice ambiguously.

Joan waved merrily after her. Across the bridge went Eunice and along the white lane to Lowfield Hall. She took the box of chocolates out of the paper bag, threw the bag over a hedge, and munched an orange cream. She wasn't displeased to have had a chat. Joan Smith was just the sort of person she got on best with, though the hint of getting her to church smacked a little of interference in her life. But she had noted something exceptionally soothing about their talk. The printed word or anything associated with it hadn't remotely come up.

But Eunice, with her television set returned and as good

as new, wouldn't have considered seeking Joan Smith out if Joan Smith had not first come to her.

This bird-like, bright-haired and bright-spirited little body was as devoured with curiosity about her fellow men as Eunice was indifferent to them. She also suffered from a particular form of paranoia. She projected her feelings on to the Lord. A devout woman must not be uncharitable, so she seldom indulged her dislike of people by straight malicious gossip. It was not she who found fault with them and hated them, but God; not she but God on whom they had inflicted imaginary injuries. Vengeance is mine, saith the Lord: I will repay. Joan Smith was merely his humble and energetic instrument.

She had long wanted to know more about the interior of Lowfield Hall and the lives of its occupants – more, that is, than she could gain by occasionally steaming open their post. Now was her chance. She had met Eunice, their initial chat had been entirely satisfactory, and here was a postcard come from Crete, come from Melinda Coverdale, and addressed to Miss E. Parchman. Joan kept it back from the regular postwoman's bag and on the Monday she took it up to the Hall herself.

Eunice was surprised and not a little put out to see her. She recoiled from the postcard as from an insect with a sting and muttered her usual defence:

'I can't see that without my glasses.'

'I'll read it to you, shall I, if I won't be intruding? "This is a super place. Temperature in the upper eighties. We have been to the Palace of Knossos where Theseus killed the Minotaur. See you soon. Melinda." How lovely. Who's this Theseus? I wonder. Must have missed that in the paper. There's always a terrible lot of fighting and killing in those places, isn't there? What a lovely kitchen! And you keep it like a new pin. Eat your dinner off the floor, couldn't you?'

Relieved and gratified, Eunice came out of herself enough to say, 'I was just going to put the kettle on.'

'Oh, no, thank you, I couldn't stop. I've left Norm all alone. Fancy her writing "Melinda" like that. I will say for her, she's no snob, though there are sides to her life distressing to the Lord in his handmaiden.' Joan uttered this last in a brisk and practical way as if God had given her his opinion while dropping in for a natter. She peered through the open door into the passage. 'Spacious, isn't it? Could I just have a peep in the drawing room?'

'If you want,' said Eunice. *'I've* no objection.'

'Oh, they wouldn't mind. We're all friends in this village. And speaking as one who has been a sinner herself, I wouldn't set myself above those who haven't found the strait gate. No, you'll never hear me say, Thank God I am not as other men are, even as this publican. Beautiful furnishings, aren't they, and in the best of taste?'

The upshot of all this was that Joan was taken on a tour of Lowfield Hall. Eunice, somewhat overawed by all this educated talk, wanted to show off what *she* could do, and Joan gratified her by frequent exclamations of delight. They went rather further than they should have done, Eunice opening Jacqueline's wardrobe to display her evening gowns. In Giles's room, Joan stared at the cork wall.

'Eccentric,' she said.

'He's just a bit of a boy,' said Eunice.

'Terrible, those spots he has, quite a disfigurement. His father's in a home for alcoholics, as of course you know.' Eunice didn't, any more than anyone else did, including Jeffrey Mont. 'He divorced her and Mr Coverdale was the corespondent, though his wife had only been dead six months. I don't sit in judgement, but I can read my Bible. "Whosoever shall marry a divorced woman, committeth adultery." What's he got that bit of paper stuck up there for?'

76

'That's always there,' said Eunice. Was she at last to dis-cover what Giles's message to her said?

She was.

In a shrill, amazed and outraged tone, Joan read aloud:

' "Warburg's friend said to Warburg, of his wife who was ill, If it should please God to take one or other of us, I shall go and live in Paris." '

This quotation from Samuel Butler had no possible ap-plication to anything in Giles's life, but he liked it and each time he read it it made him laugh.

'Blasphemous,' said Joan. 'I suppose it's something he's got to learn for school. Pity these teachers don't have more thought for a person's soul.'

So it was something he had to learn for school. By now Eunice felt quite warmly towards Joan Smith, sent by some kindly power to enlighten her and set her mind at rest.

'You won't say no to that cup of tea now, will you?' she said when, the carpet, bathroom and television set having been admired (though not, according to Joan, good enough for a superior housekeeper like yourself, more a companion really), they were once more in the kitchen.

'I shouldn't, not with Norm all on his own-io, but if you twist my arm.'

Joan Smith stayed for a further hour, during which time she told Eunice a number of lies about the Coverdales' pri-vate life, and attempted unsuccessfully to elicit from her hostess details of hers. Eunice was only a little more forth-coming than she had been at their first meeting. She wasn't going to tell this woman, helpful as she had been, all about Mum and Dad and Rainbow Street and the sweetshop, not she. Nor was she prepared to go with Joan to some prayer meeting in Nunchester on the following Sunday. What, swap her Sunday-evening spy serial for hymn-singing with a lot of cranks?

Joan didn't take offence.

'Well, I'll say thanks for the magical mystery tour and your generous hospitality. And now I must be on my way or Norm'll think I've met with an accident.'

She laughed merrily at this prospect of her husband's anxiety and drove off in the van, calling 'Cheeri-bye' all the way down the drive.

Chapter 9

The relationship between Eunice Parchman and Joan Smith was never of a lesbian nature. They bore no resemblance to the Papin sisters, who, while cook and housemaid to a mother and daughter in Le Mans, murdered their employers in 1933. Eunice had nothing in common with them except that she also was female and a servant. She was an almost sexless being, without normal or abnormal desires, whose vague restlessness over the Eu-nicey, mother of Timothy, business had long ago been allayed. As for Joan Smith, she had exhausted her sexual capacities. It is probable that like Queen Victoria in the anecdote, Eunice, for all her adventurous wanderings, did not know what lesbianism was. Joan Smith certainly knew and had very likely experimented with it, as she had experimented with most things.

For the first sixteen years of her life Joan Smith, or Skinner as she then was, led an existence which any psychologist would have seen as promising to result in a well-adjusted, worthy and responsible member of society. She was not beaten or neglected or deserted. On the contrary, she was loved, cherished and encouraged. Her father was an insurance salesman, quite prosperous. The family lived in a house which they owned in the better part of Kilburn, the parents were happily married, and Joan had three brothers older than herself who were all fond of and kind to their little sister. Mr and Mrs Skinner had longed for a daughter and been ecstatic when they got one. Because she was seldom left to her own devices but talked to and played with almost from birth, she learned to read when she was four, went happily off to school before she was five, and by the age of ten showed promise of being cleverer than any of her brothers. She passed the scholarship and went to the high school where she later gained her school certificate with the fairly unusual distinction of an exemption from matriculation, as her results were so good.

The war was on and Joan, like Eunice Parchman, had gone away from London with her school. But to foster-parents as kind and considerate as her own. For no apparent reason, suddenly and out of the blue, she walked into the local police station in Wiltshire where she accused her foster-father of raping and beating her, and she showed bruises to support this charge. Joan was found not to be a virgin. The foster-father was charged with rape but acquitted because of his sound and perfectly honest alibi. Joan was taken home by her parents, who naturally believed there had been a miscarriage of justice. But she only stayed a week before decamping to join the author of her injuries, a baker's roundsman in Salisbury. He was a married man, but he left his wife and Joan stayed with him for five years. When he went to prison for defaulting on the maintenance payments to his wife and two children, she left him and returned to London. But not to her parents, whose letters she had steadfastly refused to answer.

Another couple of years went by, during which Joan worked as a barmaid, but she was dismissed for helping herself from the till, and she drifted into a kind of suburban prostitution. She and another girl shared a couple of rooms in Shepherd's Bush where they entertained an artisan clientele who paid them unbelievably low rates for their services. From this life, when she was thirty, Joan was rescued by Norman Smith.

A weak and innocent creature, he met Joan when she went to a hairdresser's in Harlesden for a tint and perm. One side of this establishment was for the ladies, the other a barber's shop, but there was much coming and going on the part of the assistants, and Norman often stopped for a chat with Joan while she was under the dryer. She was almost the first woman he had looked at, certainly the first he had asked out. But she was so kind and sweet and friendly, he didn't feel at all intimidated. He fell violently in love with her and asked her to marry him the second time he found himself alone with her. Joan accepted with alacrity.

Norman had no idea how she had earned her living, believing her story that she had taken in typing and occasionally been a freelance secretary. They lived with his mother. After a year or two of furious daily quarrels with old Mrs Smith, Joan found the best way of keeping her quiet was to encourage her hitherto controlled fondness for the bottle. Gradually she got Mrs Smith to the stage of spending her savings on half a bottle of whisky a day.

'It would kill Norman if he found out,' said Joan.

'Don't you tell him, Joanie.'

'You'd better see you're in bed then when he comes home. That poor man idolizes you, he puts you on a pedestal. It'd break his heart to know you were boozing all day, and under his roof too.'

So old Mrs Smith, with Joan's encouragement, became a self-appointed invalid. For most of each day she was in bed with her whisky, and Joan helped matters along by crushing into the sugar in her tea three or four of the tranquillizers the doctor had prescribed for her own 'nerves'. With her mother-in-law more or less comatose, Joan returned by day to the old life and the flat in Shepherd's Bush. She made very little money at it, and her sexual encounters had become distasteful to her. A remarkable fact about Joan was that, though she had had sexual relations with hundreds of men as well as with her own husband, she had never made love for pleasure or had a 'conventional' illicit affair except with the baker's roundsman. It is hard to know why she continued as a prostitute. Out of perversity, perhaps, or as a way of defying Norman's extreme working-class respectability.

If so, it was a secret way, for he never found her out. It was she eventually who boldly and ostentatiously confessed it all to him.

And that came about as the result of her conversion. Since she was fourteen, and she was now nearly forty, she had never given a thought to religion. But all that was necessary to turn her into a raving Bible-thumper was a call at her front door by a man representing a sect called the Epiphany People.

'Not today, thanks,' said Joan, but having nothing better to do that afternoon, she glanced through the magazine, or tract, he had left on the doorstep. By one of those coincidences that are always happening, she found herself on the following day actually passing the Epiphany People's temple. Of course, it wasn't really a coincidence. She had passed it a hundred times before but had never previously noticed what it was. A prayer meeting was beginning. Out of curiosity Joan went in – and was saved.

The Epiphany People were a sect founded in California in the 1920s by a retired undertaker called Elroy Camps. Epiphany, of course, is 6 January, the day on which the Magi are traditionally supposed to have arrived in Bethlehem to bear witness to the birth of Christ and to bring him gifts. Elroy Camps and his followers saw themselves as 'wise men' to whom a special revelation had been granted: that is, they and only they had witnessed the divine manifestation, and hence only they and a select band of the chosen would find salvation. Indeed, Elroy Camps believed himself to be a reincarnation of one of the Magi and was known in the sect as Balthasar.

Astrict morality was adhered to, members of the sect must attend the temple, pay a minimum of a hundred proselytizing house calls a year, and hold to the belief that within a very short time there would be a second Epiphany in which they, the new wise men, would be chosen and the rest of the world cast into outer darkness. Their meetings were vociferous and dramatic, but merry too with tea and cakes and film shows. New members were called upon to confess their sins in public, after which the rest of the brethren would burst into spontaneous comment and end by singing hymns. Most of these had been written by Balthasar himself.

The following is an example:

As the Wise Men came riding in days long gone by,
So we ride to Jesus with hearts held up high;
Bearing our sins as they bore him presents
That shall be washed white in his holy essence.

At first it seems a mystery why all this should have made an appeal to Joan. But she had always loved drama, especially drama of a nature shocking to other people. She heard a woman confess her sins loudly proclaiming such petty errors as bilking London Transport, fraudulent practice with regard to her housekeeping money, and visits to a theatre. How much better than that could she do! She was forty, and even she could see that with her faded fair hair and fine pale skin she hadn't worn well. What next? A grim obscure domesticity in Harlesden with old Mrs Smith, or the glorious publicity the Epiphany People could give her. Besides, it might all be true. Very soon she was to believe entirely in its truth.

She made the confession of the year. It all came out. The congregation were stunned by the revelation of Joan's excesses, but she had been promised forgiveness and she got it, as much as the woman who had travelled on the Tube without a ticket got it.

Joan the faithless wife opened her heart to a stunned and disillusioned Norman. Joan the evangelist went from house to house in Harlesden and Wood Lane and Shepherd's Bush, not only distributing tracts but recounting to her listeners how, until the Lord called her, she had been a 'harlot' and a scarlet woman.

'I was arrayed in purple and scarlet colour,' said Joan on the doorstep. 'I had a golden cup in my hand full of the abominations and filthiness of my fornication. I was the hold of every unclean spirit and a cage of every unclean and hateful bird.'

It wasn't long before some wit was making snide cracks while in the barber's chair about unclean and hateful birds. In vain did Norman ask his wife to stop it. He had suffered enough in learning of her former mode of life without this. The street buzzed with it and the boys called after him as he went to work.

But how do you reproach a woman who has reformed, who counters every reproof with total agreement? 'I know that, Norm, I know I was steeped in lowness and filth. I sinned against you and the Lord. I was a lost soul, plunged in the abominations of iniquity.'

'I just wish you wouldn't tell everyone,' said Norman.

'Balthasar said there is no private atonement.'

Then old Mrs Smith died. Joan was never at home and she was left all day in a cold and filthy house. She got out of bed, fell and lay on the floor for seven hours in only a thin nightgown. That night, not long after Norman had found her, she died in hospital. Cause of death: hypothermia; she had died of exposure. Again the street buzzed, and it was not only schoolboys who called after Norman.

His mother had left him the house and a thousand pounds. Norman was one of those people – and they are legion – whose ambition is to keep a country pub or shop. He had never lived in the country or run a grocer's, but that was what he wanted. He underwent training with the post office, and at about the same time as the Coverdales bought Lowfield Hall he and Joan found themselves proprietors of Greeving Village Store – Greeving, because the only other Epiphany temple in the country was in Nunchester.

The Smiths ran the store with disastrous inefficiency. Sometimes it opened at nine, sometimes at eleven. The post office was, of course, open during its prescribed hours, but Joan (for all her virtuous protestations to Eunice) left Norman in sole charge for hours and he couldn't leave his cubby-hole behind the grille to serve other customers. Those who had been regulars drifted away. The rest, compelled through carlessness to allegiance, grumbled ferociously. Joan investigated the mails. It was her duty, she said, to find out the sinners who surrounded her. She steamed open envelopes and reglued them. Norman watched in misery and despair longing for the courage to hit her, and hoping against all odds and his own nature that he would one day find it.

They had no children and now Joan was passing through what she called an 'early change'. Considering she was fifty, it might have been thought that her menopause was neither early nor late but right on time.

'Norm and I always longed for kiddies,' she was in the habit of saying, 'but they never came. The Lord knew best, no doubt, and it's not for us to question His ways.'

No doubt, He did. One wonders what Joan Smith would have done with children if she had had them. Eaten them, perhaps.

Chapter 10

For a long time George Coverdale had suspected one of the Smiths of tampering with his post. Only a week before he went on holiday an envelope, containing a letter from his son Peter, showed a glue smear under the flap, and a parcel from the book club to which Jacqueline subscribed had obviously been opened and retied with string. But he hesitated to take action without positive proof.

He hadn't set foot in the shop or used the post office since the day, some three years before, when, in front of an interested audience of farm labourers' wives, Joan had gaily reproached him for living with a divorced woman and exhorted him to abandon his sinful life and come to God. After that he had posted his letters in Stantwich and given Joan no more than a stiff nod when he met her in the village. He would have been appalled had he known she had been in his bedroom, fingered his clothes and toured his house.

But when he and his family returned from holiday there was no sign that Eunice had defected from her established ways.

'I don't believe she's been out of the house, darling,' said Jacqueline.

'Yes, she has.' Village gossip always reached them by way of Melinda. 'Geoff told me. He got it from Mrs Higgs, the Mrs Higgs who rides the bike; she's his grandma's sister-in-law. She saw her out for a walk in Greeving.'

'Good,' said George. 'If she's happy pottering about the

village, I won't press her about the driving lessons. But if you should get it via the bush telegraph that she's got hankerings to learn, perhaps you'll let me know.'

Late summer, early autumn, and the vegetation seemed to become too much for man and nature itself to control. The flowers grew too tall and too straggly, the hedges over-brimmed with leaves, berries and tendrils of the bryony, and the wild clematis, the Old Man's Beard, cast over all its filmy fluffy cloak. Melinda went blackberrying, Jacqueline made bramble jelly. Eunice had never before seen jam being made. As far as she had known, if it didn't exactly descend like manna from heaven, at least it was only available in jars from a shop. Giles picked no blackberries, nor did he attend the Harvest Festival at St Mary's. On the cork wall he pinned a text of his own, a line that might have been written for him: *'Some say life is the thing, but I prefer reading'*, and he went on struggling through the Upanishads.

Pheasant shooting began. Eunice saw George go into the gun room, take the shotguns down from the wall and, leaving the door to the kitchen open, clean and load them. She watched with interest but in innocence, having no idea of their being of future use to her.

George cleaned and loaded both guns, but not because he had any hope of Giles accompanying him on the shoot. He had bought the second gun for his stepson, just as he had bought the fishing tackle and the fat white horse, now eating its head off down in the meadow. Three autumns of apathy and then downright opposition on Giles's part had taught George to abandon hope of making him a sportsman. So the second gun was lent to Francis Jameson-Kerr, stockbroker son of the brigadier.

Pheasants were plentiful, and from the kitchen window, then from the kitchen garden where she went to cut a cabbage, Eunice watched the three of them bag four brace and a hen bird. A brace for the Jameson-Kerrs, a brace each for Peter and Paula, the remaining birds for Lowfield Hall. Eunice wondered how long the bloodied bundles of feathers were to be hung in the back kitchen before she had the pleasure of tasting this hitherto unknown flesh. But she wasn't going to ask, not she. A week later Jacqueline roasted them, and as Eunice tucked into the thick slice of breast on her plate, three little round pellets of shot rolled out into the gravy.

The shopping was always done by Jacqueline, or a list phoned by Jacqueline to a Stantwich store and the goods later collected by George. It was a chronic source of anxiety to Eunice that one day she might be called on to phone that list, and one Tuesday in late September this happened.

The phone rang at eight in the morning. It was Lady Royston to say that she had fallen, thought she had broken her arm, and could Jacqueline drive her to hospital in Nullchester? Sir Robert had taken one car, her son the other, and then, having taken it into her head to begin picking the apple crop at the early hour of seven-thirty, she had climbed the ladder and slipped on a broken rung.

The Coverdales were still at breakfast. 'Poor darling Jessica,' said Jacqueline, 'she sounded in such pain. I'll get over there straight away. The shopping list's ready, George, so Miss Parchman can phone it through when the shop opens, and then perhaps you'll be an angel and pick it up?'

George and Giles finished their breakfast in a silence broken only by George's remarking, in the interest of being a good stepfather, that such a brilliant start to the day could only indicate rain later. Giles, who was thinking about an advertisement he had seen in *Time Out* asking for a tenth passenger in a minibus to Poona, said 'Could it?' and that he didn't know anything about meteorology. Eunice came in to clear the table.

'My wife's had to go out on an errand of mercy,' said George, made pompous by Eunice's forbidding presence, 'so perhaps you'll be good enough to get on to this number and order what's on the list.'

'Yes, sir,' said Eunice automatically.

'Ready in five minutes, Giles? Give it till after nine-thirty, will you, Miss Parchman? These shops don't keep the early hours they did in our young days.'

Eunice stared at the list. She could read the phone number and that was about all. By now George had disappeared to get the Mercedes out. Giles was upstairs. Melinda was spending the last week of her holiday with a friend in Lowestoft. The beginning of a panic stirring, Eunice thought of asking Giles to read the list to her – one reading would be enough for her memory – on the grounds that her glasses were somewhere up at the top of the house. But the excuse was too feeble, as she had an hour in which to fetch those glasses herself, and now, anyway, Giles was crossing the hall in his vague sleepwalking way, leaving the house, slamming the front door behind him. In despair, she sat down in the kitchen among the dirty dishes.

All her efforts went into rousing some spark out of that atrophied organ, her imagination. By now an inventive woman would have found ways of combating the problem. She would have said she had broken her reading glasses (and trodden on them to prove it) or feigned illness or fabricated a summons to London to the bedside of a sick relative. Eunice could only think of actually taking the list to the Stantwich store and handing the list to the manager. But how to get there? She knew there was a bus, but not where it stopped, only that the stop was two miles distant; not when it ran or where precisely it went or even the location of the shop. Presently habit compelled her to stack the dishes in the washer, wipe clean the surfaces, go upstairs to make the beds and gaze sullenly at Giles's Quote of the Month which would have had a peculiarly ironical application to herself had she been able to understand it. Nine-fifteen. Eva Baalham didn't come on Tuesdays, the milkman had already been. Not that Eunice would have dared expose herself by asking for enlightenment from these people. She would have to tell Jacqueline that she had forgotten to phone, and if Jacqueline came back in time to do it herself... She glanced up again at the cork wall, and then into her mind came a clear picture of having stood there with Joan Smith.

Joan Smith.

No very lucid plan had formed. Eunice was just as anxious for Joan Smith not to know her secret as for Eva or the milkman or Jacqueline not to know it. But Joan too had a grocer's shop, and once the list was in her hands, there might be a way. She put her best hand-knitted cardigan on over her pink cotton frock and set off for Greeving.

'Long time no see,' said Joan, sparkling. 'You are a stranger! This is Norman, my better half. Norm, this is Miss Parchman from the Hall I was telling you about.'

'Pleased to meet you,' said Norman Smith from behind his grille. Enclosed by bars, he had the look of some gloomy ruminant animal, a goat or llama perhaps, which has too long been in captivity to recall its freedom but still frets dully within its cage. His face was wedge-shaped, white and bony, his hair sandy grey. As if he were sustaining the cud-chewing image, he munched spearmint all day long. This was because Joan said he had bad breath.

'Now to what do we owe the pleasure of your visit?' said Joan. 'Don't tell me Mrs Coverdale's going to patronize our humble abode at last. That *would* be a red-letter day.'

'I've got this list.' Looking vaguely about her at the shelves, Eunice thrust the list at Joan.

'Let me see. We *have* got the plain flour and the oats, that I do know. But, my goodness, kidney beans and basil leaves and garlic!' The bad shopkeeper's excuse came to Joan's aid. 'We're waiting for them to come in,' she said. 'But, I tell you what, you read it out and I'll check what we do have.'

'No, you read it. I'll check.'

'There's me being tactless again! Ought to remember your eye trouble, didn't I? Here goes, then.'

Eunice, checking and finding only two items available, knew that she was saved, for Joan read the list out in a clear slow voice. It was enough. She bought the flour and the oats which would have to be hidden, would have to be paid for out of her own money, but what did that matter? A warm feeling for Joan, who had saved her again, welled in Eunice. Dimly she remembered feeling something like this long ago, ages ago, for her mother before Mrs Parchman became ill and dependent. Yes, she would have the cup of tea Joan was offering, and take the weight off her feet for ten minutes.

'You'll just have to phone that Stantwich place,' said Joan, who thought she saw it all, that Eunice had come to the village store off her own bat. 'Use our phone, go on. Here's your list. Got your glasses?'

Eunice had. The ones with the tortoise-shell frames. While Joan bustled about with the teacups, she made her call, almost dizzy with happiness. Appearing to read aloud what she in fact remembered brought her a pleasure comparable to, but greater than, the pride of a traveller who has one idiomatic French phrase and chances to bring it out successfully at the right time without evoking from his listener a single question. Seldom did it happen to her to *prove* she could read. And, putting the phone down, she felt towards Joan the way we feel towards those in whose presence we have demonstrated our prowess in the field where we least possess it – warm, prideful, superior yet modest, ready to be expansive. She praised the 'lovely old room', ignoring its untidy near-squalor, and she was moved so far as to compliment Joan on her hair, her floral dress and the quality of her chocolate biscuits.

'Fancy them expecting you to hump all that lot back,' said Joan who knew they hadn't. 'Well, they say he's a hard man, reaping where he has not sown and gathering where he has not stored. I'll run you home, shall I?'

'I'd be putting you out.'

'Not at all. My pleasure.' Joan marched Eunice through the shop, ignoring her husband who was peering disconsolately inside a sack as into a nosebag. The old green van started after some heavy manipulation with the choke and kicks at the accelerator. 'Home, James, and don't spare the horses!'

The van coughed its way up the lane. Joan took Eunice to the front door of Lowfield Hall. 'Now, one good turn deserves another, and I've got a little book here I want you to read.' She produced a tract entitled *God Wants You For A Wise Man*. 'And you'll pop along to our next meeting with me, won't you? Sunday night. I won't call for you, but you be in the lane at half five and I'll pick you up. OK?'

'All right,' said Eunice.

'Oh, you'll love it. We don't have a prayer book like those church people, just singing and love and uttering what comes into our hearts. And then there's tea and a chat with the brethren. God wants us to be joyful, my dear, when we have given our all to him. But for those who deny him there shall be weeping and gnashing of teeth. Did you knit your cardigan yourself? I think it's smashing. Don't forget your flour and your oats.'

Well content, Joan drove back to Norman and the store. It might seem that she had nothing to gain from friendship with Eunice Parchman, but in fact she was badly in need of a satellite in the village. Norman had become a cipher, not much more than a shell of a man since his wife's revelations of what his early married life had truly been. They hardly spoke these days, and Joan had given up pretending to her acquaintances that they were an ideal couple. Indeed, she told everyone that Norman was her cross, though one that it was her duty as his wife to bear, but that he had turned his back on God and so could be no companion for such as she. God was displeased with him. Therefore she, as his handmaid, must concur in that displeasure. These pronouncements, made publicly along with others implying that Joan had the infallibility of God's personal assistant, had put off such Higgses, Baalhams and Newsteads as might have become her friends. People said good morning to her but otherwise ostracized her. They thought she was mad, as she probably was even then.

She saw Eunice as malleable and green. And also, to do her justice, as a lost sheep who might be brought to the Nunchester fold. It would be a triumph for her, and pleasant, to have a faithful admiring attendent to introduce to the Epiphany People and be seen by unregenerate Greeving as her special pal.

Eunice, flushed with success, turned out the morning room, and was actually washing down its ivory-painted walls when Jacqueline came back.

'Heavens, what a rush! Poor Lady Royston's got a multiple fracture of her left arm. Spring-cleaning in September? You're an indefatigable worker, Miss Parchman. I hardly like to ask if you saw to my shopping list.'

'Oh, yes, madam. Mr Coverdale will pick it up at five.'

'That's marvellous. And now I'm going to have an enormous sherry before my lunch. Why don't you have a break and join me?'

But this Eunice refused. Apart from a rare glass of wine at a relative's wedding or funeral, she had never tasted alcohol. This was one of the few things she had in common with Joan Smith who, though fond enough of a gin or a Guinness in her Shepherd's Bush days, had eschewed liquor on signing the Epiphany pledge.

God Wants You For A Wise Man necessarily remained unread, but Eunice went to the meeting where no one expected her to read anything. She enjoyed the ride in Joan's van, the singing and the tea, and by the time they were back in Greeving a date had been made for her to have supper with the Smiths on Wednesday, and they were Joan and Eunice to each other. They were friends. In the sterile existence of Eunice Parchman, Mrs Samson and Annie Cole had a successor.

Melinda went back to college, George shot more pheasants, Jacqueline planted bulbs and trimmed the shrubs and cheered up Lady Royston, Giles learned gloomily that the tenth place in the bus to Poona had been filled. Leaves turned from dark green to bleached gold, the apples were all gathered and the cob nuts ripened. The cuckoo had long gone, and now the swallows and the flycatchers departed for the south.

On Greeving Green the hunt met and rode down the lane to kill two hours later in Marleigh Wood.

'Good morning, master,' said George at his gate to Sir Robert Royston, George who would call him Bob at any other time.

And 'Good morning, sir,' said Bob in his pink coat and hard hat.

October, with its false summer, its warm sadness, mists and mellow fruitfulness and sunshine turning to gold the haze that lingered over the River Beal.

Chapter 11

Melinda would have learned that when Eunice went out, as she now frequently did, it was to visit Joan Smith, and that when she set off in the dusk on Sunday evenings the Smiths' van was waiting for her at the end of the drive. But Melinda was back at college, and had returned to her father's house only once in the month since her departure. And on that one occasion she had been unusually quiet and preoccupied, not going out, but playing records or sitting silent and deep in thought. For Melinda had fallen in love.

So although every inhabitant of Greeving who was not an infant or senile followed with close interest the Parchman-Smith alliance, the Coverdales knew nothing about it. Often they didn't know that Eunice wasn't in the house, so unobtrusive was she when there. Nor did they know that when they went out Joan Smith came in and passed many a pleasant evening with Eunice, drinking tea and watching television on the top floor. Giles, of course, was invariably in. But they took care not to speak on the stairs, the thick carpet muffled the sound of an extra set of footsteps, and they passed unseen and unheard by him into Eunice's bedroom where the incessant drone of the television masked the murmur of their voices.

And yet that friendship would have foundered in its earliest days had Eunice had her way. The warmth she felt for Joan cooled when her delight over the deciphering of the shopping list subsided, and she began to look on Joan, as she had always looked on most people, as someone to be used. Not to be blackmailed for money this time, but rather to be placed in her power as Annie Cole had been, so that she could always be relied on as an interpreter and trusted not to divulge her secret if she discovered it.

It looked as if Eva Baalham had delivered Joan into her hands.

Eva was disgruntled these days because, although she now had more rewarding employment with Mrs Jameson-Kerr, her working hours at Lowfield Hall had been reduced to one morning a week. And this demotion she blamed on Eunice, who did with ease all the jobs she used to groan over and, if the truth were admitted, did them a lot better. As soon as she thought she saw a way of needling Eunice she set about doing so.

'I reckon you're very pally with that Mrs Smith then.'

'I don't know,' said Eunice.

'Always in and out of each other's places. That's what I call very pally. My cousin Meadows that's got the garage, he saw you out in her van last week. Maybe there's things about her you don't know.'

'What?' said Eunice, breaking her rule.

'Like what she was before she came here. A street woman, she was, no better than a common prostitute.' Eva wasn't going to destroy the esoteric quality of this by saying it was generally known. 'Used to go with men, and her husband never knew a thing, poor devil.'

That night Eunice was invited to the Smiths for supper. They ate what she liked and never got at Lowfield Hall, eggs and bacon and sausages and chips. Afterwards she had a chocolate bar from the shop. Norman sat silent at the table, then departed for the Blue Boar where, out of pity, some Higgs or Newstead would play darts with him. Bumper cups of tea were served. Joan leaned confidingly across the table and began to preach the gospel according to Mrs Smith. Having finished the last square of her fudge wafer, Eunice seized her opportunity.

She interrupted Joan in her louder, more commanding, voice. 'I've heard something about you.'

'Something nice, I hope,' said Joan brightly.

'Don't know about nice. That you used to go with men for money, that's what I heard.'

A kind of holy ecstasy radiated Joan's raddled face. She banged her flat bosom with her fist. 'Oh, I was a sinner!' she declaimed. 'I was scarlet with sin and steeped in the foulest mire. I went about the city as an harlot, but God called me and, lo, I heard him! I shall never forget the day I confessed my sins before the multitude of the brethren and opened my heart to my husband. With true humility, dear, I have laid bare my soul to all who would hear, so that the people may know even the blackest shall be saved. Have another cup, do.'

Amazement transfixed Eunice. No potential blackmail victim had ever behaved like this. Her respect for Joan became almost boundless and, floored, she held out her cup meekly.

Did Joan guess? Perhaps. She was a clever woman and a very experienced one. If it were so, the hoisting of Eunice with her own petard must have brought her enormous amusement without in the least alienating her. After all, she expected people to be sinners. She wasn't a Wise Man for nothing.

The yellow leaves were falling, oak and ash and elm and the redder foliage of the dogwood. What flowers that remained had been blackened by the first hard frost, and fungus grew under hedges and on fallen trees, the Oyster Mushroom and the Amethyst Agaric. Rethatching began on James Newstead's cottage, his garden filled with the golden straw from a whole wheat field.

George in dinner jacket and Jacqueline in a red silk gown embroidered with gold went to Covent Garden to see *The Clemency of Titus*, and spent the night at Paula's. The Quote of the Month was from Mallarme: 'The flesh, alas, is sad and I have read all the books'. But Giles, far from having read all the books, was deep in Poe. If, as seemed likely, he was never going to make it to India, he might ask Melinda to share a flat with him when they had completed their education. A Gothic mansion flat was what he had in mind, in West Kensington, say, a kind of diminutive House of Usher with floors of ebon blackness and feeble gleams of encrimsoned light making their way through the trellised panes.

But Melinda, unknown to him, was in love. Jonathan Dexter was his name and he was reading modern languages. George Coverdale had often wondered, though never spoken his thoughts aloud even to Jacqueline, whether his younger daughter was as innocent as her mother had been at her age. But he doubted it, and was resigned to her having followed the current trend of permissiveness. He would, in fact, have been surprised and pleased had he known Melinda was still a virgin, though anxious if he had guessed how near she was to changing that irrevocable condition.

Now that the ice was, as it were, broken, Eunice often went out walking. As she had roved London, so she roved the villages, marching from Cocklefield to Marleigh, Marleigh to Cattingham, through the leaf-strewn lanes, and as St Luke's Little Summer gave place to the deep of autumn, daring the still dry footpaths that crossed the fields and skirted the woods. She walked purposelessly, not pausing to look, through breaks in the trees, at the long blue vistas of wooded slopes and gentle valleys, hardly noticing the countryside at all. Here it was the same for her as it had been in London. She walked to satisfy some craving for freedom and to use up that energy housework could not exhaust.

She and Joan Smith never communicated by phone. Joan would arrive in the van when she was sure Lowfield Hall was empty but for Eunice. Whatever friend she visited, Jacqueline must pass through Greeving, and she seldom passed without being observed by Joan from the village store. And then Joan would drive up to the Hall, make her way in through the gun room without knocking, and within two minutes Eunice had the kettle on.

'Her life's just one round of amusement. Sherry-partying with that Mrs Cairne she is this morning. One can just imagine what goes on in the mind of God when he looks down on that sort of thing. The wicked shall flourish like the green bay tree, but in the morning they were not, nay, they were not to be found. I've got four calls to make in Cocklefield this morning, dear, so I won't stop a minute.' By calls Joan didn't mean store or postal deliveries, but proselytizing visits. As usual, she was armed with a stack of tracts, including a new one got up to look like a comic and artfully entitled *Follow My Star*.

So fervid an Epiphany Person was she that often when Eunice called at the store during her walks only Norman was found to be in charge. And then from behind the bars of his cage, he shook his head lugubriously.

'She's off out somewhere.'

But sometimes Eunice called in time to be taken with Joan on her rounds, and from the passenger seat in the van she watched her friend preaching on cottage doorsteps.

'I wonder if you have time to spare today to glance at a little book I've brought...'

Or around the council estates that clung to the fringe of each village, red-brick boxes screened from the ancient settlement by a barrier of conifers. Occasionally a naïve householder asked Joan in, and then she was gone some time. But more often the door was shut in her face and she would return to the van, radiated with the glow of martyrdom.

'I admire the way you take it,' said Eunice. 'I'd give them as good as I got.'

'The Lord requires humility of his servants, Eun. Remember there are some who will be carried by the angels into Abraham's bosom and some who will be tormented by the flame. Don't let me forget to stop at Meadows', we're nearly out of petrol.'

They presented a strange sight, those two, to the indignant watcher as she dropped *Follow My Star* into her dustbin. Joan so spindly with bones like those of a starved child pictured in a charity appeal, her religion having done nothing to conquer her ingrained habit, almost unconscious now, of getting herself up in whore's garb: short skirt, black 'glass' stockings, down-at-heel patent shoes, great shiny handbag and fleecy white jacket with big shoulders. Her hair was like an inverted bird's nest, if birds ever built with golden wire, and on her pinched little face the make-up was rose and blue and scarlet.

Eunice might have been chosen as the perfect foil to her. She had added to her wardrobe since coming to Lowfield Hall only such garments as she had knitted herself, and on those chilly autumn days she wore a round woolly cap and a scarf of dark grey-blue. In her thick maroon-coloured coat she towered above Joan, and the contrast was best seen when they walked side by side, Joan teetering and taking small rapid steps, Eunice Junoesque with her erect carriage and steady stride.

In her heart, each thought the other looked a fool, but this did not alienate them. Friendship often prospers best when one party is sure she has an ascendancy over the other. Without letting on, Eunice thought Joan brilliantly clever, to be relied on for help whenever she might be confronted by reading matter, but mutton dressed as silly young lamb all the same, a hopeless housewife and a slattern. Without letting on, Joan saw Eunice as eminently respectable, a possible bodyguard too if Norman should ever attempt to carry out his feeble threat of beating her up, but why dress like a policewoman?

Joan made Eunice presents of chocolate each time she came to the shop. Eunice had knitted Joan a pair of gloves in her favourite salmon pink, and was thinking of beginning on a jumper.

All Saints, 1 November, was Jacqueline's forty-third birthday. George gave her a sheepskin jacket, Giles a record of Mozart concert arias. Melinda sent a card with a scrawled promise of 'something nice when I get around to coming home'. The parcel, containing a new novel, which arrived from Peter and Audrey, had obviously been opened and resealed. George marched off to Greeving Post Office and Village Store and complained to Norman Smith. But what to say in answer to Norman's defence that the book was half out of its wrappings on arrival, and that his wife had repacked it herself for safety's sake? George could only nod and say he wouldn't take it further – for the present.

That week he went for his annual check-up to Dr Crutchley and was told his blood pressure was up, nothing to worry about but better go on these tablets. George wasn't a nervous man or one who easily panicked, but he decided he had better make his will, a proceeding he had been procrastinating about for years. It was this will which has given rise to the litigation that still continues, that keeps Lowfield Hall ownerless and deserted, that has soured the lives of Peter Coverdale and Paula Caswall and keeps the tragedy fresh in their minds. But it was carefully drawn up, with all forethought. Who then could have foreseen what would happen on St Valentine's Day? What lawyer, however circumspect, could have imagined a massacre at peaceful Lowfield Hall?

A copy of the will was shown to Jacqueline when she got home from a meeting of the parish council.

' "To my beloved wife, Jacqueline Louise Coverdale," ' she read aloud, ' "the whole of my property known as Lowfield Hall, Greeving, in the County of Suffolk, unencumbered, and to be hers and her heirs' and successors' in perpetuity." Oh, darling, "beloved wife"! I'm glad you put that.'

'What else?' said George.

'But shouldn't it just be for my life? I've got all the money Daddy left me and what I got for my house, and there'd be your life assurance.'

'Yes, and that's why I've willed all my investments to the girls and Peter. But I want you to have the house, you love it so. Besides, I hate those pettifogging arrangements where the widow only gets a life interest. She's a non-paying tenant to a bunch of people who can't wait for her to die.'

'Your children wouldn't be like that.'

'I don't think they would, Jackie, but the will stands. If you predecease me, I've directed that the Hall is to be sold after my death and the proceeds divided between my heirs.'

Jacqueline looked up at him. 'I hope I do.'

'Hope you do what, darling?'

'Die first. That's what I mind about your being older than me, that you're almost certain to die first. I might be a widow for years, I can't bear the thought of it, I can't imagine a single day without you.'

George kissed her. 'Let's *not* talk of wills and graves and epitaphs,' he said, so they talked about the parish council meeting instead, and fund-raising for the new village hall, and Jacqueline forgot the hope she had expressed.

It was not destined to be gratified, though she was to be a widow for only fifteen minutes.

Chapter 12

The Epiphany Temple in Nunchester is on North Hill just above the cattle market. Therefore, it is not necessary when driving there from Greeving to pass through the town, and Joan Smith could make the journey in twenty minutes. Eunice enjoyed the Sunday-night meetings. Hymn sheets were provided, but as anyone knows who has tried to give the impression that he has the Church of England morning service off by heart (actually to use the Prayer Book being to betray unpardonable ignorance) it is quite easy to mouth what other people are mouthing and muffle one's lack of knowledge in folded hands brought to the lips. Besides, Eunice had only to hear a hymn once to know it for ever, and soon, in her strong contralto, she was singing with the best of them:

'Gold is the colour of our Lord above,
And frankincense the perfume of His love;
Myrrh is the ointment, which with might and main,
He pours down from heaven to heal us of our pain.'

Elroy Camps was no Herbert or Keble.

After the hymns and some spontaneous confessing – almost as good as television, this bit – the brethren had tea and biscuits and watched films about black or brown Epiphany People struggling on in remote places (*in partibus infidelium,* as it were) or delivering the Epistle of Balthasar to famine-stricken persons too weak to resist. Also there was friendly gossip, mostly about worldly people who hadn't seen the light, but uttered in a pious way and shoving the onus of censure and blame off on to God. Certainly the brethren honoured the precept of Come unto Me, all ye that are heavy laden, and I will give ye rest.

On the whole, they were and are a jolly lot. They sing and laugh and enter with gusto into their own confessions and those of new converts. They talk of God as if he were a trendy headmaster who likes the senior boys to call him by his Christian name. Their hymns are not unlike pop songs and their tracts are lively with comic strips. The idea of the elect being Wise Men who follow a star is not a bad one. The Camps cult would probably have been latched on to by young people of the Jesus freak kind but for its two insuperable drawbacks distasteful to anyone under forty – and to most people over forty, come to that. One is its total embargo on sexual activity, whether the parties are married or not; the other its emphasis on vengeance against the infidel, which means any non-Epiphany Person, a vengeance that is not necessarily left to God but may be carried out by the chosen as his instruments. In practice, of course, the brethren do not go about beating up their heretical neighbours, but the general impression is that if they do they will be praised rather than censured. After all, if God is their headmaster they are all prefects.

Eunice absorbed little of this doctrine which, in any case was implicit rather than proclaimed. She enjoyed the social life, almost the first she had ever known. The brethren were her contemporaries or her seniors; no one questioned her or attempted to interfere unpleasantly with her life or manipulated her into corners where she would be expected to read. They were friendly and cajoling and liberal with tea and biscuits and fruit cake because, of course, they saw her as a future convert. But Eunice was determined never to convert, and for her usual reason for not doing something.

She wouldn't have minded the confessing because she would have confessed nothing beyond the usual run of evil thoughts and ambitions, but once she had taken that step she would be obliged to make the duty calls. And she knew only too well from her visits with Joan what that entailed. Reading. Drawing the attention of the visited to points in *Follow My Star*, picking appropriate bits out of the Bible, arguing with frequent reference to the printed word.

'I'll think about it,' she said in her ponderous way when Joan pressed her. 'It's a big step.'

'A step towards Bethlehem which you would never regret. The Son of Man cometh like a thief in the night, but the foolish virgin has let her lamp go out. Remember that, Eun.'

This exchange took place one raw damp afternoon when Eunice had walked down to the village store for a cup of tea, a chat, and to collect her week's supply of chocolate bars which had again become an indispensable part of her diet. As they came out of the shop together, Jacqueline also came out of Mrs Cairne's house where she had been on some Women's Institute matter. They didn't notice her, but she saw them, and although Joan only came as far as the triangle of turf, it was obvious that what was taking place was no ordinary farewell of shopkeeper to customer. Joan was laughing in her shrill way, and while doing so she stuck out her hand and gave Eunice one of those playful pushes on the arm women of her kind do give to women friends in the course of making a joking reproof. Then Eunice walked off in the direction of the Hall, turning twice to wave to Joan who waved back quite frenziedly.

Jacqueline started her car and caught Eunice up just beyond the bridge.

'I didn't know you were friendly with Mrs Smith,' she said when Eunice, somewhat reluctantly, had got in beside her.

'I see a bit of her,' said Eunice.

There seemed no answer to make to this. Jacqueline felt she couldn't very well dictate to her housekeeper as to whom she chose for her friends. Not in these days. It wasn't Eunice's afternoon off, but they had all forgotten about those prescribed afternoons and evenings off since their holiday. She went out when she chose. After all, why not? It wasn't as if she neglected her duties at Lowfield Hall, far from it. But Jacqueline, who until now had had no fault to find with her housekeeper, who had been aghast when George, five months before, had voiced faint qualms, was suddenly made uncomfortable. Eunice sat beside her, eating chocolates. She didn't eat them noisily or messily, but wasn't it odd that she should be eating them at all, munching silently and not offering the bag? Nothing would have induced Jacqueline to eat a chocolate under any circumstances, but still... And hob-nobbing with Mrs Smith as if they were fast friends? Some awareness that George, if told of it, would concur rather too emphatically in her own view, stopped her mentioning it to him.

Instead, with her own particular brand of feminine perverseness, she praised Eunice to the skies that evening, pointing out how beautifully all the silver was polished.

In Galwich, Melinda Coverdale, wise or foolish, had surrendered her virginity to Jonathan Dexter. It happened after they had shared a bottle of wine in his room and Melinda had missed the last bus. Of course, the wine and the bus were not accidental happenings. Both had been inwardly speculating about them all the evening, but they were handy excuses for Melinda next day. She hardly needed consolation, though, for she was very happy, seeing Jonathan every day and spending most nights in his room. Sweet's Anglo-Saxon and Baugh on the history of the English language weren't so much as glanced at for a fortnight, and as for Goethe, Jonathan had found his Elective Affinities elsewhere.

At Lowfield Hall Jacqueline had made four Christmas puddings, one of which would be sent to the Caswalls who couldn't face the upheaval of bringing two infants to Greeving for the holiday. She wondered what to buy for George, but George had everything – and so had she. Eunice watched her ice the Christmas cake, and Jacqueline waited for her to make some remark, reminiscing or sentimental, when the plaster Santa Claus, the robins and the holly leaves were fixed to the frosting, but Eunice said merely that she hoped the cake would be large enough, and she only said that when asked for her opinion.

Disillusionment over India had killed oriental religion for Giles. It would never, anyway, have fitted in with his plans for himself and Melinda. He saw them sharing their flat, devout Catholics both, but going through agonies to maintain their chaste and continent condition. Perhaps he would become a priest, and if Melinda were to enter a convent, they might – say twice a year – have special dispensations to meet and, soberly garbed, have tea together in some humble cafe, not daring to touch hands. Or like Lancelot and Guinevere, but without the preceding pleasures, encounter each other across a cathedral nave, gaze long and hard, then part without a word. Even to him this fantasy seemed somewhat extreme. Before becoming a priest he must become a Catholic, and he was looking around Stantwich for someone to give him instruction. Latin and Greek would have their uses, so Virgil and Sophocles received more attention. He put that line from Chesterton up on the wall, the bit about the twitch upon the thread, and he was reading Newman.

Winter had stripped bare the woods and the hedges, and screaming gulls followed Mr Meadows' plough. The magical light of Suffolk became wan and opalescent, and the sky, as the earth turned its farthest from the sun, almost green with a streaking of long butter-coloured clouds. Blood is nipped and ways be foul and nightly sings the staring owl. From cottage chimneys the smoke of log fires rose in long grey plumes.

'What are you doing for our Lord's Nativity?' said Joan in the tone of someone asking a friend to a birthday party.

'Pardon?' said Eunice.

'Christmas.'

'Stopping at the Hall. They've got folks coming.'

'It does seem a shame you having to spend the Lord's birthday among a bunch of sinners. There's nothing to choose between the lot of them. Mrs Higgs that rides the bike, she told Norm that Giles is consorting with Catholic priests. God doesn't want you contaminated by the likes of that, dear.'

'He's only a bit of a boy,' said Eunice.

'You can't say that about his adulterous stepfather. Coming in here and accusing Norm of tampering with his post! Oh, how far will the infidel go in his persecution of the elect! Why don't you come to us? We'll be very quiet, of course, but I think I can guarantee you a goodly refection and the company of loving friends.'

Eunice said she would. They were drinking tea at the time in Joan's squalid parlour, and the third loving friend, in the shape of Norman Smith, came in looking for his dinner. Instead of fetching it, Joan went off into a repetition of her confession which the slightest mention of others who had offended in a similar, or assumed by her to be similar, way was likely to evoke.

'You've led a pure life, Eun, so you can't know what mine has been, delivering up my body, the temple of the Lord, to the riff-raff of Shepherd's Bush. Submitting myself un-heeding to the filth of their demands, every kind of disgusting desire which I wouldn't name to a single lady agreed to for the sake of the hard cash that my husband couldn't adequately provide.'

Courage came at last to Norman. He had had two whiskies in the Blue Boar. He advanced on Joan and hit her in the face. She is a very small woman, and she fell off her chair, making glugging noises.

Eunice rose ponderously to her feet. She went up to Norman and took him by the throat. She held the chicken skin of his throat like she might hold a hank of wool, and she laid her other hand hard on his shoulder.

'You leave her alone.'

'I've got to listen to that, have I?'

'If you don't want me shaking the life out of you.' Eunice suited the action to the threat. It was for her a wholly delightful experience and one which she vaguely wondered she hadn't indulged in before. Norman cringed and shuddered as she shook him, his eyes popped and his mouth fell open.

Joan's trust in her as a bodyguard had been justified.

She sat up and said dramatically, 'With God's help, you have saved my life!'

'Load of rubbish,' said Norman. He broke free and stood rubbing his throat. 'You make me sick, the pair of you. Couple of old witches.'

Joan crawled back into her chair to examine her injuries, a ladder in one of her stockings and what would develop into a mild black eye. Norman hadn't really hurt her. He was too feeble and, basically, too frightened of her to do that. Nor had she struck her head when she fell. But something happened to her as the result of that weak blow and that fall. Psychological perhaps, rather than physical – and connected also with the glandular changes of the menopause? Whatever it was, Joan was altered. It was gradual, of course, it hardly showed itself on that evening except in a brighter glitter in her eyes and a shriller note to her voice. But that evening was the beginning of it. She had reached the edge of a pit in which was nothing short of raving madness, and she teetered there on the brink until, two months later, whipped-up fanaticism toppled her over.

Chapter 13

'We'll go in the front way,' said Eunice, back from the Epiphany meeting. She sensed that Joan would be unwelcome at the Hall, though Joan had never told her so and had, on the contrary, at the time of her first visit said that the Coverdales would not object to her exploring their house because 'we're all friends in this village'. Eunice had never heard from George or Jacqueline a hint of their suspicions as to their post, but somehow, by means of her peculiar and often unreliable intuition, she knew – just as she was aware that had she brought home with her Mrs Higgs of bicycle fame or Mrs Jim Meadows, these ladies would have been graciously received by any Coverdale who chanced to see them.

Joan didn't mean to stop long, having only come to have her measurements taken for some secret plan of Eunice's to do with a Christmas present. They were already on the top flight when Giles's bedroom door opened and he came out.

'Looks as if he was backward to me,' said Joan in Eunice's room. She flounced out of her white coat. 'Bit retarded, if you know what I mean.'

'He won't say a word,' said Eunice.

But there she was wrong.

Giles wouldn't have said a word if he hadn't been asked. That wasn't his way. He had gone downstairs to fetch his Greek dictionary which he thought he had left in the morning room. There he found his mother alone, watching a concert of chamber music on the television. George had gone out for half an hour to discuss with the brigadier how to counter a proposal to build four new houses on a piece of land near the river bridge.

Jacqueline looked up and smiled. 'Oh, darling,' she said, 'it's you.'

'Mmm,' said Giles, groping under a pile of Sunday papers for his Liddell and Scott.

'I thought I heard someone on the stairs, but I imagined it was Miss Parchman coming in.'

Occasionally it flashed across Giles's brain that he ought, perhaps once a day, to utter a whole sentence rather than a monosyllable to his mother. He was quite fond of her really. So he forced himself. He stood up, spiky-haired, spotty, myopic, the mad young professor weighted down by a learned tome.

'You did,' he said in his vague abstracted way, 'with that old woman from the shop.'

'What old woman? What on earth do you mean, Giles?'

Giles didn't know the names of anyone in the village. He never went there if he could help it. 'The lunatic woman with the yellow hair,' he said.

'Mrs Smith?'

Giles nodded and wandered off towards the door, his dictionary already open, muttering something that sounded to Jacqueline like 'anathema, anathema'. Her patience with him snapped. Briefly she forgot what he had said, or the significance of it.

'Oh, Giles, darling, you must *not* call people lunatics. Giles, wait a minute, *please*. Couldn't you possibly stop down here with us sometimes in the evenings? I mean, you can't have that much homework, and you know you can do it with your eyes shut. You're turning into a hermit, you'll get like that man who sat on top of a pillar!'

He nodded again. The admonition, the request, the flattery, passed over him unheard. He considered very seriously, rubbing one of his spots.

At last he said, 'St Simeon Stylites,' and walked slowly out, leaving the door open.

Exasperated, Jacqueline slammed it. For a while, her concert being over, she sat thinking how much she loved her son, how proud she was of his scholastic attainments, how ambitious for him – and how much happier she would have been had he been more like George's children. And then, because it was useless trying to do anything about Giles, who would surely one day become normal and nice, she returned to what he had said. Joan Smith. But before she could dwell much on it, George came in.

'Well, I think we shall put a spoke in their wheel. Either this place is scheduled as an Area of Natural Beauty or else it isn't. If it comes to a public inquiry we shall all have to get together and brief counsel. You say the parish council are very much opposed?'

'Yes,' said Jacqueline. 'George, Mrs Smith from the store is upstairs. She came in with Miss Parchman.'

'I thought I saw the Smiths' van in the lane. How very unfortunate.'

'Darling, I don't want her here. I know it sounds silly, but it makes me feel quite ill to think of her being here. She goes about telling people Jeffrey divorced me and named you, and that he's a dipsomaniac and all sorts of things. And I *know* she opened the last letter I had from Audrey.'

'It doesn't sound silly at all. The woman's a menace. Did you say anything?'

'I didn't see her. Giles did.'

George opened the door. He did so at the precise moment Eunice and Joan were creeping down the stairs in the dark. He put on the light, walked along the passage and confronted them.

'Good evening, Mrs Smith.'

Eunice was abashed, but not Joan. 'Oh, hallo, Mr Coverdale. Long time no see. Bitterly cold, isn't it? But you can't expect anything else at this time of year.'

George opened the front door for her and held it wide. 'Good night,' he said shortly.

'Cheeri-bye!' Joan scuttled off, giggling, a schoolgirl who has been caught out of bounds.

Thoughtfully, he closed the door. When he turned round Eunice had disappeared. But in the morning before breakfast, he went to her in the kitchen. This time she wasn't doing miracles with his dress shirt. She was making toast. He had thought of her as shy, and had blamed all her oddities on her shyness, but now he was aware, as he had been once six months before, of the disagreeable atmosphere that prevailed wherever she was. She turned round to look at him like an ill-tempered cow had once looked at him when he went too close to its calf. She didn't say good morning, she didn't say a word, for she knew why he had come. A violent dislike of her seized him, and he wanted the kitchen back in its disordered state, the saucepans still not washed from the night before, an au pair muddling through.

'I'm afraid I've got something rather unpleasant to say, Miss Parchman, so I'll make it as brief as possible. My wife and I don't wish to interfere in your personal life, you are at liberty to make what friends you choose. But you must understand we cannot have Mrs Smith in this house.'

He was pompous, poor George. But who wouldn't have been in the circumstances?

'She doesn't do any harm,' said Eunice, and something stopped her calling him sir. She was never again to call George sir or Jacqueline madam.

'I must be the best judge of that. You have a right to know the grounds of my objection to her. I don't think one can seriously say a person does no harm when she is known to spread malicious slanders and, well, to abuse her husband's position as postmaster. That's all. I can't, of course, prevent your visiting Mrs Smith in her own home. That is another matter. But I will not have her here.'

114

Eunice asked no questions, offered no defence. She shrugged her massive shoulders, turned away and pulled out the grill pan on which three slices of toast were burnt black.

George didn't wait. But as he left the kitchen he was sure he heard her say, 'Now look what you've made me do!'

He talked about it in the car to Giles, because Giles was there and his mind was full of it and, anyway, he was always racking his mind for something to say to the boy.

'You know, I've been very loth to admit it, but there's something definitely unpleasant about that woman. Perhaps I shouldn't be saying this to you, but you're grown up, you must be aware of it, feel it. I don't quite know the word I want to describe her.'

'Repellent,' said Giles.

'That's exactly it!' George was so delighted not only to have been supplied with this adjective but also because it had been supplied, quite forthcomingly, by Giles, that he took his eyes off the road and had to swerve sharply to avoid hitting Mr Meadows' ancient labrador which was ambling along in the middle of the lane. 'Look where you're going, you daft old thing,' he called after it in a kind of affectionate relief. 'Repellent, that's the word. Yes, she sends shivers up my spine. But what's to be done, Giles old boy? Put up with it, I suppose?'

'Mmm.'

'I daresay it's just made me a bit nervous. I'm very likely exaggerating. She's taken an enormous burden of work off your mother's shoulders.'

Giles said 'Mmm' again, opened his case and began muttering bits out of Ovid. Disappointed, but well aware that there was to be no repetition of that inspired contribution to this very one-sided discussion, George sighed and gave up. But a very nasty thought had struck him. If Eunice had been able to drive, if she had been driving this car five minutes before, he was intuitively certain she wouldn't have swerved to avoid the dog, or if it had been a child, to avoid that either.

Jacqueline left a note in the kitchen to say she would be out all day. She didn't want to see Eunice who was upstairs doing the 'children's' bathroom. It was a pity, she now thought, that Giles had told her about seeing Joan Smith, and an even greater one that she had been so impulsive as to tell George. Eunice might leave, or threaten to leave. Jacqueline drove off through the village to the Jameson-Kerrs' house, and when she saw the smeary windows, the dust lying everywhere, and her friend's rough red hands, she told herself that she must keep her servant at any cost and that the occasional presence of Joan Smith was a small price to pay.

Joan saw the car go by and put on her fleecy coat.

'Off to the Hall, I suppose?' said Norman. 'I wonder you don't live up there with Miss Frankenstein.'

Though she had once done so, Joan no longer unloaded her biblical claptrap on to her husband. He was the only person she knew who escaped it. 'Don't you say a word against her! If it wasn't for her I might be dead.'

Munching gum, Norman peered into one of his sacks. 'Stupid fuss to make about a little tap.'

'If it wasn't for her,' shouted Joan, with a flash of wit, 'you wouldn't be looking at mailbags, you'd be sewing them.'

She jumped into the van and roared up over the bridge. Eunice was in the kitchen, loading the washing machine with sheets and shirts and table linen.

'I saw her go off in her car, so I thought I'd pop up. Did you get into a row last night?'

'Don't know about a row.' Eunice closed the lid of the machine and put the kettle on. 'He says you're not to come here.'

Joan's reaction was loud and violent. 'I knew it! I could see it coming a mile off. It's not the first time the servants of God have been persecuted, Eun, and it won't be the last.' She swept out a spindly arm, narrowly missing the milk jug. 'Look what you do for them! Isn't the labourer in the vineyard worthy of his hire? He'd have to pay you twice what you're getting if you didn't have that poky room up there, but he doesn't think of that. He's no more than a landlord, and since when's a landlord got a right to interfere with a person's friends?' Her voice rose to a tremulous shriek. 'Even his own daughter goes about saying he's a fascist. Even his kinsmen stand afar from him. Woe to him whom the Lord despiseth!'

Unmoved by any of this, Eunice stared stolidly at the boiling kettle. No surge of love for Joan rose in her, no impulse of loyalty affected her. She was untouched by any of that passion which heats one when one's basic rights are threatened. She simply felt, as she had been feeling ever since the night before, that her life was being interfered with. At last she said, in her heavy level way:

'I don't mean to take any notice.'

Joan let out a shrill laugh. She was enormously pleased. She bubbled with excitement. 'That's right, dear, that's my Eun. You make him knuckle under. You show him it's not everyone that goeth when he says go and cometh when he says come.'

'I'll make the tea,' said Eunice. 'Have a look at that note she's left, will you? I've left my glasses upstairs.'

Chapter 14

During term Melinda had only twice been home, but now that term had come to an end. Jonathan was going to Cornwall with his parents until after the New Year and she had been invited to go with them, but it would have taken more than being in love to keep Melinda from Lowfield Hall at Christmas. With promises to phone every day, to write often, they parted and Melinda got on the train for Stantwich.

Again it was Geoff Baalham who picked her up at Gallows Corner. No great coincidence this, as Geoff was always returning from his egg delivery round at about this time. But on 18 December it was dark at five, the windows of the van were closed and the heater on, and Melinda wore an embroidered Afghan coat and a big fur hat. Only the boots were the same.

'Hi, Melinda. You *are* a stranger. Don't tell me it's your studies been keeping you up in Galwich.'

'What else?'

'A new boyfriend, or that's what I heard.'

'You just can't keep anything to yourself in this place, can you? Now tell me what's new.'

'Barbara's expecting. There'll be another little Baalham come July. Can you see me as a dad, Melinda?'

'You'll be marvellous. I'm so glad, Geoff. Mind you give my love to Barbara.'

'Of course I will,' said Geoff. 'Now, what else? My Auntie Nellie had a nasty fall off her bike and she's laid up with a bad foot.

Did you hear about your dad throwing Mrs Smith out of the house?'

'You don't mean it!'

'It's a fact. He caught her sneaking down the stairs with your lady help and he told her not to come there again, and then he threw her out. She's got bruises all down her side, or so I heard.'

'He's a terrible fascist, isn't he? But that's *awful*.'

'Don't know about awful, not when you think what she says about your ma and opens their letters, according to what I hear. Well, here's where I leave you, and tell your ma I'll drop the eggs by first thing Monday.'

Geoff drove home to Barbara and the chickens thinking what a nice girl Melinda was – that crazy fur hat! – and that the boyfriend was a lucky guy.

'You didn't really throw Mrs Smith out and bruise her all down her side, did you?' said Melinda, bursting into the morning room where George, the carpet covered with a sheet, was cleaning his guns because it was too cold in the gun room.

'That's a nice way to greet your father when you haven't seen him for a month.' George got up and gave her a kiss. 'You're looking well. How's the boyfriend? Now what's all this about me assaulting Mrs Smith?'

'Geoff Baalham said you had.'

'Ridiculous nonsense. I never touched the woman. I didn't even speak to her beyond saying good night. You ought to know village gossip by this time, Melinda.'

Melinda threw her hat on to a chair. 'But you did say she mustn't come here again, Daddy?'

'Certainly I did.'

'Oh, poor Miss Parchman! It's awfully feudal interfering with her friendships. We were so worried because she didn't know anyone or go anywhere, and now she's got a friend you won't have her in the house. It's a *shame*.'

'Melinda...' George began.

119

'I shall be very nice to her. I'm going to be very kind and caring. I can't bear to think of her not having a single friend.'

'It's her married friend I object to,' said George wickedly, and he laughed when Melinda flounced out.

So that evening Melinda began on a disaster course that was to lead directly to her death and that of her father, her stepmother and her stepbrother. She embarked on it because she was in love. It is not so much true that all the world loves a lover as that a lover loves all the world. Melinda was moved by her love to bestow love and happiness, but it was tragic for her that Eunice Parchman was her object.

After dinner she jumped up from the table and, to Jacqueline's astonishment, helped Eunice to clear. It was to Eunice's astonishment too, and to her dismay. She wanted to get the dishes done in time to watch her Los Angeles cop serial at eight, and now here was this great tomboy bouncing about and mixing gravied plates up with water glasses. She wasn't going to speak, not she, and perhaps the girl would take the hint and go away.

A kind of delicacy, an awareness of the tasteful thing, underlay Melinda's extrovert ways, and she sensed that it would be disloyal to her father to mention the events of the previous Sunday. So she began on a different tack. She could hardly have chosen a worse subject, but for one.

'Your first name's Eunice, isn't it, Miss Parchman?'

'Yes,' said Eunice.

'It's a biblical name, but of course you know that. But I think it's Greek really. Eu-nicey or maybe Eunikey. I'll have to ask Giles. I didn't do Greek at school.'

A dish was banged violently into the machine. Melinda, herself a habitual dish-banger, took no notice. She sat on the table.

'I'll look it up. The Epistle to Timothy, I think. Of course it is! Eu-nicey, mother of Timothy.'

'You're sitting on my tea towel,' said Eunice.

'Oh, sorry. I'll have to check, but I think it says something about thy mother Eunice and thy grandmother Lois. I don't suppose your mother's name is Lois, is it?'

'Edith.'

'Now that must be Anglo-Saxon. Names are fascinating, aren't they? I love mine. I think my parents had very good taste calling us Peter and Paula and Melinda. Peter's coming next week, you'll like him. If you'd had a son, would you have called him Timothy?'

'I don't know,' said Eunice, wondering why she was being subjected to this persecution. Had George Coverdale put her up to it? Or was it just done to mock? If not, why did that great tomboy keep smiling and laughing? She wiped all the surfaces viciously and drained the sink.

'What's your favourite name then?' said her inquisitor.

Eunice had never thought about it. The only names she knew were those of her relatives, her few acquaintances and those she had heard spoken on television. From this last, in desperation she selected, recalling her hero whose latest adventure she would miss if she didn't get a move on.

'Steve,' she said, and hanging up her tea towel, marched out of the kitchen. It had been an intellectual effort which left her quite exhausted.

Melinda was not dissatisfied. Poor old Parchman was obviously sulking over the Joan Smith business, but she would get over that. The ice had been broken, and Melinda hoped confidently for a rapport to have grown up between them before the end of her holiday.

'Eu-nee-kay,' said Giles when she asked him, and, 'There was this man, you see, who got drunk at a party, and he was staggering home at about three in the morning when he landed up in the entrance to a block of flats. Well, he looked at all the names by the bells, and there was one called S. T. Paul. So he rang that bell, and when the guy came down, all cross and sleepy in his pyjamas, the man said, "Tell me, did you ever get any replies to your letters?'" He let out a great bellow of laughter at his own joke, then abruptly became doleful. Maybe he shouldn't tell jokes like that with his conversion in view.

'You're crazy, Step,' said Melinda. She didn't appreciate, was never to appreciate, that she was the only person to whom her stepbrother ever uttered more than one isolated sentence. Her mind was on Eunice whom she sought out, armed with the Bible, next day with a dictionary of proper names. She lent her magazines, took her the evening paper George brought home, and obligingly ran upstairs to fetch her glasses when Eunice said, as she always did, that she hadn't got them with her.

Eunice was harassed almost beyond bearing. It was bad enough that Melinda and Giles were about the house all day so that Joan Smith couldn't come to see her. But now Melinda was always in her kitchen or following her about 'like a dog', as she told Joan. And she was perpetually on tenterhooks what with those books and papers constantly being thrust under her nose – which she didn't tell Joan.

'Of course you know what all that amounts to, don't you, Eun? They're ashamed of their wicked behaviour, and they've put that girl up to soft-soaping you.'

'I don't know,' said Eunice. 'She gets on my nerves.'

Her nerves were playing her up, as she put it to herself, in a way they had never done before. But she was powerless to deal with Melinda, that warm unsnubbable girl. And once or twice, while Melinda was haranguing her about names or the Bible or Christmas or family histories, she wondered what would happen if she were to pick up one of those long kitchen knives and use it. Not, of course, Eunice being Eunice, what the Coverdales would do or what would become of her, but just the immediate consequence – that tongue silenced, blood spreading over and staining that white neck.

On the 23rd Peter and Audrey Coverdale arrived.

Peter was a tall pleasant-looking man who favoured his mother rather than his father. He was thirty-one. He and his wife were childless, from choice probably, for Audrey was a career woman, chief librarian at the university where he had a post as lecturer in political economy. Audrey was particularly fond of Jacqueline. She was a well-dressed elegant bluestocking, four years older than her husband, which made her only seven years Jacqueline's junior. Before training as a librarian she had been at the Royal Academy of Music, which Jacqueline had attended before her first marriage. The two women read the same kind of books, shared a passionate love of Mozartian and pre-Mozartian opera, loved fashion and talking about clothes. They corresponded regularly, Audrey's letters being among those examined by Joan Smith.

They hadn't been in the house more than ten minutes when Melinda insisted on taking them to the kitchen and introducing them to Eunice.

'She's a member of this household. It's awfully fascist to treat her like a bit of kitchen equipment.'

Eunice shook hands.

'Will you be going away for Christmas, Miss Parchman?' said Audrey, who prided herself, as Jacqueline did, on having a fund of small-talk suitable for persons in every rank of life.

'No,' said Eunice.

'What a shame! Not for us, of course. Your loss will be our gain. But one does like to be with one's family at Christmas.'

Eunice turned her back and got the teacups out.

'Where did you get that awful woman?' Audrey said to Jacqueline later. 'My dear, she's creepy. She's not human.'

Jacqueline flushed as if she personally had been insulted. 'You're as bad as George. I don't want to make a friend of my servant, I want her the way she is, marvellously efficient and unobtrusive. I can tell you, she really knows her job.'

'So do boa constrictors,' said Audrey.

And thus they came to Christmas.

George and Melinda brought holly in to decorate Lowfield Hall, and from the drawing-room chandelier hung a bunch of mistletoe, the gift of Mr Meadows in whose oaks it grew. More than a hundred cards came for the Coverdales, and these were suspended on strings in a cunning arrangement fixed up by Melinda. Giles received only two personal cards, one from his father and one from an uncle, and these, in his opinion, were so hideous that he declined to put them up on his cork wall where the Quote of the Month was: 'To love oneself is the beginning of a lifelong romance.' Melinda made paper chains, bright red and emerald and shocking blue and chrome yellow, exactly the kind of chains she had made every year for fifteen years. Jacqueline took much the same view of them as her son did of his cards, but not for the world would she have said so.

On the Day itself the drawing room was grandly festive. The men wore suits, the women floor-length gowns. Jacqueline was in cream velvet, Melinda in a 1920s creation, rather draggled dark blue crêpe de Chine embroidered with beads which she bought in the Oxfam shop. They opened their presents, strewing the carpet with coloured paper and glitter. While Jacqueline unwrapped the gold bracelet that was George's gift, and Giles looked with something nearing enthusiasm on an unabridged Gibbon in six volumes, Melinda opened the parcel from her father.

It was a tape recorder.

Chapter 15

Everyone was drinking champagne, even Giles. He had been prevailed upon by his mother to come downstairs, and was morosely resigned to staying downstairs all day. And it would be worse tomorrow when they would be having a party. In this view Melinda concurred – all those cairns and curs and roisterers – and she sat on the floor next to him, telling him how wonderful Jonathan was. Giles didn't much mind this. Byron, after all, was never perturbed by the existence of Colonel Leigh, and Christmas would be bearable if such conclaves with Melinda became the rule. He fancied that the others had noticed their closeness and were overawed by the mystery of it.

Far from noticing anything about her son except that he was there for once, Jacqueline was thinking about the one absent member of the household.

'I really do feel,' she said, 'that we ought to ask Miss Parchman to sit down to lunch with us.'

A spontaneous groan from all but Melinda.

'A female Banquo,' said Audrey, and her husband remarked that Christmas was supposed to be for merry-making.

'And for peace and goodwill,' said George. 'I don't find the woman personally congenial, as you all know, but Christmas is Christmas and it's not pleasant to think of her eating her lunch out there on her own.'

'Darling, I'm so glad you agree with me. I'll go and ask her and then I'll lay another place.'

But Eunice was not to be found. She had tidied the kitchen, prepared the vegetables, and gone off to the village store. There in the parlour, undecorated by holly or paper garlands, she and Joan and a gloomy sullen Norman ate roast chicken, frozen peas and canned potatoes, followed by a Christmas pudding from the shop. Eunice enjoyed her meal, though she would have liked sausages as well. Joan had cooked some sausages but had forgotten to serve them, and Norman, made suspicious by a peculiar smell, found them mouldering in the grill pan a week later. They drank water, and afterwards strong tea. Norman had got some beer in, but this Joan had deposited in the bin just before the dustmen called. She was in raptures over the salmon-pink jumper Eunice had knitted for her, rushed away to put it on, and preened about in it, striking grotesque model-girl attitudes in front of the fingermarked mirror. Eunice received an enormous box of chocolates and a fruit cake from stock.

'You'll come back tomorrow, won't you, dear?' said Joan.

And so it happened that Eunice also spent Boxing Day with the Smiths, leaving Jacqueline to cope with food and drink for the thirty guests who came that evening. And the effect on Jacqueline was curious, twofold. It was as if she were back in the old days when the entire burden of the household work had been on her shoulders, and in Eunice's absence she appreciated her almost more than when she was there. This was what it would be like permanently if Eunice were to leave. And yet for the first time she saw her housekeeper as George and Audrey and Peter saw her, as uncouth and boorish, a woman who came and went as she pleased and who saw the Coverdales as so dependent on her that she held them in the hollow of her hand.

The New Year passed, and Peter and Audrey went home. They had asked Melinda to go back with them for the last week of her holiday, but Melinda had refused. She was a very worried girl.

Each day that passed made her more anxious. She lost her sparkle, moped about the house, and said no to all the invitations she got from her village friends. George and Jacqueline thought she was missing Jonathan and tactfully they asked no questions.

For this Melinda was deeply thankful. If what she feared was true – and it must be true now – they would have to know sometime. Perhaps it might be possible to get through this, or out of this, without George ever suspecting. Children understand their parents as little as parents understand their children. Melinda had had a happy childhood and a sympathetic devoted father, but her way of thinking was infected by the attitude of her friends to their parents. Parents were bigoted, prudish, moralistic. Therefore hers must be, and no personal experience triumphed over this conviction. She guessed she was George's favourite child. All the worse. He would be the more bitterly disappointed and disillusioned if he knew, and his idealistic love for her turned to disgust. She imagined his face, stern and yet incredulous, if he were even to suspect such a thing of his youngest child, his little girl. Poor Melinda. She would have been flabbergasted had she known that George had long supposed her relationship with Jonathan to be a fully sexual one, regretted it, but accepted it philosophically as long as he could believe there was love and trust between them.

Every day, of course, she had been having long phone conversations with Jonathan – George was to be faced with a daunting bill – but so far she hadn't breathed a word. Now, however, on 4 January, she knew she must tell him. This wasn't as bad as telling her father would be, but bad enough. Her experience of this kind of revelation had been culled from novel and magazine reading and from old wives' gossip in the village. When you told the man he stopped caring for you, he dropped you, didn't want to know, or at best shouldered his responsibility while implying it was all your fault. But she had to tell him. She couldn't go on carrying this frightening secret another day on her own, especially as, that morning, she had been violently sick on waking.

She waited until George had gone to work and Jacqueline and Giles to Nunchester in the second car, Jacqueline supposing that while she was shopping her son would be visiting a friend – a friend at last! though, in fact, he was to receive his first instruction from Father Madigan. Eunice was upstairs making beds. There were three telephones at Lowfield Hall, one in the morning room, an extension in the hall and another extension by Jacqueline's bed. Melinda chose the morning-room phone, but while she was getting enough courage together to make her call, it rang. Jonathan.

'Hold on a minute, Jon,' she said. 'I want to close the door.'

It was at that precise moment, while Jonathan was holding the line and had briefly laid down the receiver to light a cigarette while Melinda was closing the morning-room door, that Eunice lifted the receiver on Jacqueline's bedroom extension. She wasn't spying. She was too uninterested in Melinda and too repelled by her attentions deliberately to eavesdrop. She picked up the receiver because you cannot properly dust a telephone without doing so. But as soon as she heard Melinda's first words she was aware that it would be prudent to listen.

'Oh, Jon, something awful! I'll come straight out with it, though I'm scared stiff to tell you. I'm pregnant. I know I am. I was sick this morning and I'm nearly two weeks overdue. It'll be frightful if Daddy or Jackie find out, Daddy would be so let down, he'd hate me, and what am I going to *do*?'

She was nearly crying. Choked by tears that would soon spill over, she waited for the stunned silence. Jonathan said quite calmly, 'Well, you've got two alternatives, Mel.'

'Have I? You tell me. I can't think of anything but just running away and dying!'

'Don't be so wet, lovey. You can have an abortion if you really want...'

'Then they'd be sure to know. If I couldn't get it on the National Health and I had to have money or they wanted to know my next of kin or...'

By now Melinda was hysterical. Like almost all women in her particular situation, she was in a blind unreasoning panic, fighting against the bars of the trap that was her own body. Eunice screwed up her nose. She couldn't stand that, lot of fuss and nonsense. And perhaps it was something else as well, some unconscious sting of envy or bitterness that made her lay the receiver down. Lay it down, not replace it. It would be unwise to do that until after their conversation was over. She moved away to dust the dressing table, and thus she missed the rest.

I don't like the idea of abortion,' said Jonathan. 'Do get yourself together, Mel, and calm down. Listen, I want to marry you, anyway. Only I thought we ought to wait till we've got our degrees and jobs and whatever. But it doesn't matter. Let's get married as soon as we can.'

'Oh, Jon, I do love you! Could we? I'd have to tell them even though we're both over eighteen, but, Jon...'

'But nothing. We'll get married and have our baby and it'll be great. You come up to Galwich tomorrow instead of next week and I'll hitch back and you can stay with me and we'll make plans, OK?'

It was very much OK with Melinda who, having wept with despair, was now bubbling with joy. She would go to Jonathan next day and tell George she'd be staying with her friend in Lowestoft. It was awful lying to him, but all in a good cause, better that than let him know, wait till they'd published the banns or got the licence. And so on. She wasn't sick on 5 January. Before she had packed her case she knew her fears had been groundless, the symptoms having resulted from anxiety and their cessation from relief. But she went just the same and took a taxi from the station to Jonathan's flat, so impatient to tell him she wasn't going to have a baby after all.

Being in possession of someone else's secret reminded Eunice of the days of blackmailing the homosexual and, of course, Annie Cole. It was a piece of information which Joan Smith would have delighted to hear, Joan who rather resented the way Eunice never told her anything about the private lives of the Coverdales. She wasn't going to tell her this either. A secret shared is no longer a secret especially when it has been imparted to someone like Joan Smith who would whisper it to what customers she still retained in no time. No, Eunice was going to keep this locked in her board-like bosom, for you never knew when it might come in useful.

So, on the following night, when she climbed into the van that was waiting for her in Greeving Lane, she gave nothing away.

'I noticed the Coverdale girl went back to her college yesterday,' said Joan. 'Bit early, wasn't it? All set for a week of unbridled cohabitation with that boyfriend she's got, I daresay. She'll come to a bad end. Mr Coverdale's just the sort of hard man to cast his own flesh and blood out of the house if he thought they'd been committing fornication.'

'I don't know,' said Eunice.

Twelfth Night, 6 January, Epiphany, is the greatest day in the calendar for the disciples of Elroy Camps. The meeting was sensational – two really uninhibited confessions, one of them rivalling Joan's own, an extempore prayer shrieked by Joan at the top of her voice, five hymns.

'Follow the star!
Follow the star!
The Wise Men turn not back.
Across the desert, hills or foam,
The star will lead them to their home
White or brown or black!'

They ate seed cake and drank tea. Joan became more and more

excited until, eventually, she had a kind of seizure. She fell on the floor, uttering prophecies as the spirit moved her, and waving her arms and legs about. Two of the women had to take her into a side room and calm her down, though on the whole the Epiphany People were more gratified than dismayed by this performance.

Only Mrs Elder Barnstaple, a sensible woman who came to the meetings for her husband's sake, seemed disquieted. But she supposed Joan was 'putting it on'. Not one of that company guessed at the truth, that Joan Smith was daily growing more and more demented and her hold on reality was becoming increasingly tenuous. She was like a weak swimmer whose grasp of a slippery rock has never been firm. Now her fingers were sliding helplessly down its surface, and currents of madness were drawing her into the whirlpool.

She hardly spoke as she drove the van home, but from time to time she let out little bursts of giggles like the chucklings of something unhuman that haunted those long pitch-dark lanes.

Chapter 16

Bleak midwinter, and the frosty wind made moan. Eva Baalham said that the evenings were drawing out, and this was true but not that one would notice. The first snow fell in Greeving, a dusting of snow that thawed and froze again.

On the cork wall, from St Augustine: 'Too late loved I Thee, O Thou Beauty so ancient and so new, too late came I to love Thee!' For Giles the road to Rome was not entirely satisfactory as Father Madigan, accustomed until recently to Tipperary peasants, expected from him their ignorance and their blind faith. He didn't seem to understand that Giles knew more Greek and Latin than he and had got through Aquinas before he was sixteen. In Galwich Melinda was blissfully happy with Jonathan. They were still going to get married but not until she had taken her degree in fifteen months' time. To this end, because she would need a good job, she was working quite hard, between making love and making plans at her Chaucer and her Gower.

The cold pale sun pursued a low arc across a cold pale sky, aquamarine and clear, or appeared as a puddle of light in a high grey field of cloud.

19 January was Eunice's forty-eighth birthday. She noted its occurrence but she told no one, not even Joan. It was years since anyone had sent her a card or given her a present on that day.

She was alone in the house. At eleven the phone rang. Eunice didn't like answering the phone, she wasn't used to it and it alarmed her. After wondering whether it might not be better to ignore it, she picked up the receiver reluctantly and said hello.

The call was from George. Tin Box Coverdale had recently changed their public-relations consultants, and a director of the new company was coming to lunch, to be followed by a tour of the factory. George had prepared a short history of the firm which had been established by his grandfather – and had left his notes at home.

He had a cold and his voice was thick and hoarse. 'The papers I want you to find are in the writing desk in the morning room, Miss Parchman. I'm not sure where, but the sheets are clipped together and headed in block capitals: Coverdale Enterprises from 1895 to the Present Day.'

Eunice said nothing.

'Now I'd appreciate it if you'd hunt them out.' George let out an explosive sneeze. 'I beg your pardon. Where was I? Oh, yes. A driver from here is already on his way, and I want you to put the papers into a large envelope and give them to him when he comes.'

'All right,' said Eunice hopelessly.

'I'll hold the line. Have a look now, will you? And come back and tell me when you've found them.'

The desk was full of papers, many of them clipped together and all headed with something or other. Eunice hesitated, then replaced the receiver without speaking to George again. Immediately the phone rang. She didn't answer it. She went upstairs and hid in her own room. The phone rang four more times and then the doorbell. Eunice didn't answer that either. Although she wasn't celebrating her birthday it did strike her that it was very disagreeable having this happen today of all days. A person's birthday ought to be nice and peaceful, not upset by this kind of thing.

George couldn't understand what had happened. The driver came back empty-handed, the consultant left without the Coverdale history. George made a sixth call and at last got hold of his wife who had been in Nunchester having her hair tinted. No, Miss Parchman wasn't ill and had just gone out for a walk. The first thing he did when he got home was find the papers on the very top of the pile in the writing desk.

'What happened, Miss Parchman? It was of vital importance to me to have those papers.'

'I couldn't find them,' said Eunice, laying the dining table, not looking at him.

'But they were on the top. I can't understand how you could miss them. My driver wasted an hour coming over here. And surely, even if you couldn't find them, you could have come back and told me.'

'They cut us off.'

George knew that was a lie. 'I rang back four times.'

'It never rang,' said Eunice, and she turned on him her small face, which now seemed to have increased in size, to have swollen with resentment. Hours of brooding had filled her with gall, and now she used to him the tone her father had so often heard in the last weeks of his life. 'I don't know anything about any of it.' For her, she was quite voluble. 'It's no good asking me because I don't know.' The blood crept up her throat and broke in a dark flush across her face. She turned her back on him.

George walked out of the room, impotent in the face of this refusal to take responsibility, to apologize or even discuss it. His head was thick with his cold and felt as if stuffed with wet wool. Jacqueline was making up her face in front of her dressing-table mirror.

'She's not a secretary, darling,' she said, echoing the words he had used to her when she had hesitated about engaging Eunice. 'You mustn't expect too much of her.'

'Too much! Is it too much to ask someone to find four clearly labelled sheets of paper and hand them over to a driver? Besides, it isn't that which I mind so much. I never really knew what dumb insolence meant before, it was just a phrase. I know now. She doesn't give the number or our name when she answers the phone. If a pig could say "Hallo" it would sound just like Miss Parchman.'

Jacqueline laughed, smudging her mascara.

'And to put the phone down on me! Why didn't she answer when I called back? Of course the phone rang, it's just nonsense to say it didn't. And she was positively rude to me when I spoke to her about it.'

'I've noticed she doesn't like doing things which are – well, outside what she thinks of as her province. It's always the same. If I leave her a note she'll do what it asks but a bit truculently, I always think, and she doesn't like making phone calls or answering the phone.' She spoke quite blithely as if laughing off 'men's nonsense', humouring and soothing him because his cold was now worse than hers.

George hesitated, put his hand on her shoulder. 'It's no good, Jackie, she'll have to go.'

'Oh, no, George!' Jacqueline spun round on her stool. 'I can't do without her. You can't ask that of me just because she let you down over those papers.'

'It isn't just that. It's her insolence and the way she looks at us. Have you noticed she never calls us by our names? And she's dropped that sir and madam. Not that I care about that, I'm not a snob,' said George, who did and was, 'but I can't put up with bad manners and lying.'

'George, please give her one more chance. What would I do without her? I can't face the thought of it.'

'There are other servants.'

'Yes, old Eva and au pairs,' said Jacqueline bitterly. 'I had some idea what it would be like at our Christmas party. I didn't enjoy it if you did. I was doing the food all day and running around all night. I don't think I spoke to anyone except to ask if they wanted another drink.'

'And for that I have to put up with a servant who would have been a credit to the staff at Auschwitz?'

'One more chance, George, *please*.'

He capitulated. Jacqueline could always win him over. Could he pay too high a price, he asked himself, to see his beloved wife happy and relaxed and beautiful? Could he pay too much for peace and domestic comfort and a well-run elegant home? Was there anything he wouldn't part with for that?

Except my life, he might have answered, except my life.

George intended to react by taking a firm line with Eunice in accordance with his calling, to manage and direct her. He wasn't a weak man or a coward, and he had never approved the maxim that it is better to ignore unpleasantness and pretend that it does not exist. She must be admonished when she returned his smile and his 'Good morning' with a scowl and a grunt, or he would have a quiet talk with her and elicit from her what the trouble was and how they had failed.

He admonished her only once, and then jocularly. 'Can't you manage a smile when I speak to you, Miss Parchman? I don't know what I've done to deserve that grim look.'

Beseechingly, Jacqueline's eyes met his. Eunice took no notice apart from slightly lifting her shoulders. After that he said no more. He knew what would happen if he tried a tête-à-tête with her. 'There's nothing wrong. It's no use talking about it because there's nothing.' But he realized, if Jacqueline did not, that they were conciliating Eunice Parchman, allowing her to manage and direct them. For Jacqueline's sake and to his own self-disgust he found himself smiling fatuously at his housekeeper whenever they encountered each other, asking her if her room was warm enough, if she had enough free time, and once if she would *mind* staying in on a certain evening when they had guests for dinner. His warmth was met by not a shred of reciprocation.

136

February came in with a snowstorm.

Only in pictures and on television had Eunice seen real country snow before as against the slush which clogged the gutters of Tooting. It had never occurred to her that snow was something that could bother people or change their lives. On the morning of Monday, 1 February, George was up before she was with an unwilling sleepy Giles, clearing two channels in the long drive for the wheels of the Mercedes. The first light had brought Mr Meadows out with his snow plough into the lane. A shovel and boots and sacks were put into the car's boot, and George and Giles set off for Stantwich with the air of Arctic explorers.

Against a livid sky the great flakes whirled, and the landscape was blanketed but for the dark demarcations of hedges and the isolated blot of a skeleton tree. No going out for Jacqueline that day or the next or the next. She phoned to cancel her appointment with the hairdresser, her lunch with Paula, the evening engagements. Eva Baalham didn't bother to phone and say she wasn't coming. She just didn't come. You took that sort of thing for granted in East Anglia in February.

So Jacqueline was imprisoned with Eunice Parchman. Just as she was afraid to use her car, so were her neighbours afraid to call on her. Once she would have seen the coming of the snow as a possible topic of conversation between herself and Eunice, but now she knew better than to try. Eunice accepted the snow as she accepted rain and wind and sunshine. She swept the paving outside the gun-room door and the front steps without comment. Silently, she went about her work. When Jacqueline, unable to repress herself, exclaimed with relief at the sound of George's car successfully returned through the thickening drifts, she reacted no more than if this had been a normal day of ordinary weather.

And Jacqueline began to see George's point of view. Being

snowbound with Eunice was more than disconcerting; it was oppressive, almost sinister. She marched doggedly through the rooms with her duster and her polishing cloths. Once, when Jacqueline was seated at the desk writing to Audrey, the half-filled sheet of paper was lifted silently from under her nose while a duster was wiped slowly across the surface of inlaid leather and rosewood. It was as if, Jacqueline said later to her husband, she were a deaf patient in a home for the handicapped and Eunice a wardmaid. And even when the work was done, and Eunice departed upstairs to watch afternoon serials, she felt that it was not the snow alone which pressed a ponderous weight on the upper regions of Lowfield Hall. She found herself treading carefully, closing doors discreetly, sometimes just standing in the strange white light that is uniquely the reflection thrown back from snow gleaming, marmoreal and cold.

She was not to know, never dreamed, that Eunice was far more afraid of her than she was intimidated by Eunice; that the incident of the Coverdale History papers had made her retreat totally into her shell, for if she were to speak or allow them to speak to her, that arch enemy of hers, the printed word, would rise up and assail her. Reading in an armchair pulled close to a radiator, reading to please Eunice and keep clear of her, Jacqueline never guessed that she could have done nothing to please Eunice less or arouse her more to hatred.

Every evening that week she needed twice her usual allowance of sherry to relax her before dinner.

'Is it worth it?' said George.

'I talked to Mary Cairne on the phone today. She said she'd put up with positive abuse, let alone dumb insolence, to have a servant like Miss P.'

George kissed his wife, but he couldn't resist a dig. 'Let her try it then. It's nice to know Miss P.'ll have somewhere to go when I sack her.'

But he didn't sack her, and on Thursday, 4 February, something happened to distract them from their discontentment with their housekeeper.

Chapter 17

Things were getting too much for Norman Smith. He also was snowbound with a fellow-being who was uncongenial to him, only the fellow-being was his wife.

Norman had often in the past told Joan she was mad, but in much the same way as Melinda Coverdale told Giles Mont he was mad. He didn't intend to imply she was insane. But now he was sure she literally was mad. They still shared a bed. They belonged in that category of married people who share a bed without thinking about it, who would have shared a bed even if they were not on speaking terms. But often now Norman woke in the night to find Joan absent, and then he heard her in some other part of the house laughing to herself, laughing maniacally, or singing snatches of Epiphany hymns or reciting prophecies in a shrill uneven voice. She had ceased altogether to clean the house or dust the goods in the shop or sweep the shop floor. And each morning she bedizened herself in bits of bizarre clothing saved from her Shepherd's Bush days, her face painted like a clown's.

She ought to see a doctor. Norman knew quite well that she was in need of treatment for her mind. A psychiatrist was the sort of doctor she ought to see, but how to get her to one? How to go about it? Dr Crutchley held surgery twice a week in Greeving in a couple of rooms in a converted cottage. Norman knew Joan wouldn't go of her own inclination, and he couldn't imagine going *for* her. What, sit in that waiting room among coughing and snuffling Meadowses and Baalhams and Eleighs, and then explain to a tired and harassed doctor that his wife sang in the night and bawled bits from the Bible at his customers and wore knee socks and short skirts like a young girl?

Besides, the worst manifestation of her madness he couldn't confess to anyone.

Lately she seemed to think she had a right, godlike or as God's censor, to investigate any of the mail that passed through Greeving Post Office. He couldn't keep the mail sacks from her. He tried locking them up in the outside lavatory, but she broke the lock with a hammer. And now she was an expert at steaming open envelopes. He winced and trembled when he heard her telling Mrs Higgs that God had punished Alan and Pat Newstead by killing their only grandchild, information Joan had culled out of a letter from the distraught father. And when she imparted to Mr Meadows of the garage that George Coverdale was in debt to his wine merchant, he waited till the shop was empty and then he struck her in the face. Joan only screamed at him. God would have vengeance on him, God would make him a leper and an outcast who dared not show his face in the haunts of men.

This was one of her prophecies which was to prove only too true.

On Friday, 5 February, when the thaw had begun and the lane between Greeving and Lowfield Hall could be negotiated without a struggle, George Coverdale walked into the village store at nine in the morning. That is, he walked in after he had banged peremptorily on the front door and fetched Norman, who was still at breakfast, out to open up.

'You're early, Mr Coverdale,' said Norman nervously. It was seldom that George had set foot on that threshold, and Norman knew his coming boded ill.

'In my opinion, nine is not early. It's the time I usually reach my place of business, and if I shan't do so this morning it's because the matter I have to discuss with you is too serious to postpone.'

'Oh, yes?' Norman might have stood up to George, but he quailed when Joan, her yellow hair in curlers, her skin-and-bone body wrapped in a dirty red dressing gown, appeared in the doorway.

George took an envelope from his briefcase. 'This letter has been opened and resealed,' he said, and he paused. It was horrible to him to think Joan Smith spreading about the village that his wine merchant was threatening him with proceedings. And it was made all the more horrible by the fact that the letter was the result of a computer mistake. George, having paid his bill in early December when it was due, had argued the whole thing out with the retailer by phone and obtained a fulsome apology for his error. But he scorned to defend himself to these people. 'There are smears of glue on the flap,' he said, 'and inside I found a hair which I venture to suggest comes from the head of your wife.'

'I don't know anything about it,' Norman muttered. He had unwittingly used Eunice Parchman's phrasing, and this inflamed George.

'Perhaps the postmaster at Stantwich will. I intend to write to him today. I shall lay the whole matter before him, not forgetting previous occasions when I have had cause for suspicion, and I shall demand an official inquiry.'

'I can't stop you.'

'Very true. I merely felt it was just to tell you what I mean to do so that you have warning in advance. Good morning.'

All this time Joan had said nothing. But now, as George moved towards the door, distastefully eyeing the dusty packets of cornflakes and baskets of shrunken mouldy vegetables, she darted forward like a spider or a crab homing on its prey. She stood between George and the door, against the door, her stick-like arms spread against the glass, the

142

red wool sleeves falling back from flesh where the subcutaneous tissue had wasted away. She lifted her head and screamed at him:

'Generation of vipers! Whoremonger! Adulterous beast! Woe to the ungodly and the fornicators!'

'Let me pass, Mrs Smith,' said George levelly. Not for nothing had he seen service under fire in the Western Desert.

'What shall be done unto thee, thou false tongue? Sharp arrows of the mighty with coals of juniper.' Joan waved her fist in his face. 'God will punish the rich man who taketh away the livelihood of the poor. God will destroy him in his high places.' Her face was suffused with blood, her eyes white with the pupils cast up.

'Will you get your wife out of my way, Mr Smith!' said George, enraged.

Norman shrugged. He was afraid of her and powerless.

'Then l will. And if you care to sue me for assault, you're welcome.'

He pushed Joan and got the door open. Outside in the car, Giles, the least involved of people, was actually watching with interest. Joan, only temporarily worsted, ran after George and seized his coat, shouting gibberish, her dressing gown flapping in the icy wind. And by now Mrs Cairne had appeared at her window, Mr Meadows by his petrol pumps. George had never been so embarrassed in his life, he was shaking with distaste and repulsion. The whole scene was revolting to him. If he had witnessed it in the street, an angry man, a half-dressed woman clinging to his coat, shouting abuse at him, he would have turned the other way, vanished as fast as possible. And here he was, one of the protagonists.

'Be quiet, take your hands off me,' he found himself shouting back at her. 'This is outrageous!'

And then at last Norman Smith did come out and get

hold of his wife and manhandled her back into the shop. Afterwards, Meadows of the garage said he slapped her, but George didn't wait to see. With what shreds of dignity remained to him, he got into the car and drove off. For once he was glad of Giles's detachment. The boy was smiling distantly. 'Lunatic,' he said, before lapsing back into his own mysterious thoughts.

The incident upset George for the day. But he wrote his letter to the Stantwich postmaster without mentioning the scene of the morning or even that he had particular grounds for suspecting the Smiths.

'Let's hope we're going to have a quiet weekend,' he said to Jacqueline. 'What with battling to work through all this snow every day, and then this fracas this morning, I feel I've had enough. We're not going anywhere, are we, or having anyone in?'

'Just to the Archers tomorrow afternoon, darling.'

'Tea with the Rector,' said George, 'is just the kind of somniferous non-event I can do with at present.'

Melinda was not expected home, and Giles didn't count. It was rather like having a harmless resident ghost, Jacqueline sometimes thought sadly. It stalked the place, but it didn't bother you or damage things, and on the whole it kept quietly to the confines of the haunted room. She wondered from whose writings he had taken the Quote of the Month: 'I hope never again to commit a mortal sin, nor even a venial one, if I can help it.'

It was the last quotation Giles was ever to pin to his cork wall, and perhaps it was appropriate that the lines he had chosen, from Charles the Seventh of France, were said to be their author's dying words.

As it happened, Melinda did come home. Since 5 January she hadn't been back to Lowfield Hall, and her conscience was troubling her. Of course she would go home for the 13th, for that was George's birthday, but it seemed awful to stay away for five weeks. Also there was the matter of the tape recorder. George's present was her most prized possession, and because of it she was the envy of her college friends. Melinda didn't like to say no to people who asked to borrow it, but when someone took it to a folk concert, and afterwards left it all night in an unlocked car, she thought the time had come to remove it from harm's way.

Without having told anyone she was coming, she arrived in Stantwich as the dull red sun was setting, and at Gallows Corner after dark. She was just a little too late for Geoff Baalham, who had passed that way ten minutes before, and it was Mrs Jameson-Kerr who picked her up and told her George and Jacqueline had gone to tea at the Rectory.

Melinda went into the house through the gun room and immediately upstairs to find Giles. But Giles also was out. He had taken the Ford and, after a session with Father Madigan, gone to the cinema. The house was warm, spotless, exquisitely tidy and silent. Silent, that is, but for the muted tumult throbbing through the first-floor ceilings from Eunice Parchman's television. Melinda put the tape recorder on her chest of drawers. She changed into a robe she had made herself out of an Indian bedspread, put a shawl over her shoulders and a string of limpet shells round her neck, and, well pleased with the result, went down to the morning room. There she found a stack of new magazines which she took into the kitchen. Ten minutes later Eunice, coming down to remove from the deep-freeze a chicken casserole for the Coverdales' supper, found her seated at the table with a magazine open in front of her.

Melinda got up courteously. 'Hallo, Miss Parchman. How are you? Would you like a cup of tea? I've just made it.'

'I don't mind,' said Eunice, the nearest she ever got to a gracious acceptance of any offer. She frowned. 'They're not expecting you.'

'I do live here, it's my home,' was what Melinda might have said, but she was not a prickly or defensive girl. Besides, here was an opportunity to go on being nice to Miss Parchman whom she had neglected along with her family since the New Year. So she smiled and said she had made her decision on the spur of the moment, and did Miss Parchman take milk and sugar?

Eunice nodded. The magazine on the table intimidated her as much as a spider might have intimidated another woman. She hoped Melinda would concentrate on it and shut up while she drank her tea which she rather regretted accepting. But it was evident that Melinda intended to concentrate on it only with her participation. She turned the pages, keeping up a running commentary, looking up from time to time with a smile for Eunice and even passing her the magazine for her to look at a picture.

'I don't like those mid-calf-length skirts, do you? Oh, look at the way that girl has done her eyes! It must take hours, I shouldn't have the patience. All those forties fashions are coming back. Did they really dress like that when you were young? Did you wear bright red lipstick and stockings? I've never possessed a pair of stockings,'

Eunice who still wore them and who had never possessed a pair of tights, said she wasn't much for dress. Lot of nonsense, she said.

'Oh, I think it's fun.' Melinda turned the page. 'Here's a questionnaire. "Twenty Questions to Test if You're Really in Love." I must do it, though I know I am. Now, let's see. Have you got a pencil or a pen or something? '

A firm shake of the head from Eunice.

'I've got a pen in my bag.' This battered holdall, literally a carpet bag made out of Turkey rug, Melinda had dumped in the gun room. Eunice, watching her fetch it, hoped she would take bag, pen and magazine elsewhere, but Melinda returned to her place at the table. 'Now, Question One: Would you rather be with him than... Oh, I can see the answers at the bottom, that's no good. I'll tell you what, you ask me the questions and tick whether I get three marks or two or one or none at all. OK?'

'I haven't got my glasses,' said Eunice.

'Yes, you have. They're in your pocket.'

And they were. The tortoise-shell ones, the pair the Coverdales knew as her reading glasses, were sticking out of the right-hand pocket of her overall. Eunice didn't put them on. She did nothing, for she didn't know what to do. She couldn't say she was too busy – busy with what? – and nearly half a pint of hot tea remained in the mug Melinda had given her.

'Here.' Melinda passed her the magazine. 'Please do. It'll be fun.'

Eunice took it in both hands, and stumbled from memory through that first line Melinda had read. 'Would you rather be with him than...' She stopped.

Melinda reached across and picked the glasses out of her pocket. Eunice was cornered. A flush darkened her face to a deep wine colour. She looked up at the girl and her underlip trembled.

'What is it?' There was a let-out here if only Eunice had known it. For, instantly, Melinda jumped to a conclusion. Miss Parchman had reacted rather like this before, when asked what name she would have given her son if she had had one. Obviously there was something in her past that was still painful, and she, very tactlessly, had again touched the scar of that ancient disappointed love. Poor Miss Parchman who had once loved someone and was now an old maid. 'I didn't mean to upset you,' she said gently. 'I'm sorry if I said something to hurt you.'

Eunice didn't answer. She didn't know what on earth the girl was talking about. But Melinda took her silence as a sign of unhappiness, and she was seized by a need to do something to make things all right again, to distract Eunice's mind. 'I really am sorry. Let's do the quiz on the opposite page, shall we? It's all about how good a housewife one is. You do it for me and see how hopeless I am, and then I'll do it for you. I bet you get top marks.' Melinda held up the glasses for Eunice to take them.

And now Eunice should have made capital out of Melinda's misapprehension. Nothing more would have been needed but for her to say yes, Melinda had upset her, and to have walked with dignity out of the room. Such conduct would have won for her the dismayed sympathy of all the Coverdales and have supplied George with his answer. What was the root cause of Miss Parchman's sullenness and depression? A womanly sorrow, a lost love. But Eunice had never been able to manipulate people because she didn't understand them or the assumptions they made and the conclusions they drew. She understood only that she was on the brink of having her disability discovered, and because of the awful crushing domination of that disability, she thought she was nearer to that brink than she actually was. She thought Melinda already guessed, and that was why, having mockingly said she was sorry, she was trying to test her out to confirm her assumption.

The glasses, held between Melinda's finger and thumb, hovered between the two women. Eunice made no move to take them. She was trying to think. What to do, how to get out of it, what desperate measure she could seize on. Puzzled, Melinda let her hand fall, and as she did so, she looked through them from a short distance and saw that they were of plain glass. Her eyes went to Eunice's flushed face, her blank stare, and pieces of the puzzle, hitherto inexplicable – the way she never read a book, looked at a paper, left a note, got a letter – fell into place.

'Miss Parchman,' she said quietly, 'are you dyslexic?'

Vaguely, Eunice thought this must be the name of some eye disease. 'Pardon?' she said in swelling hope.

'I'm sorry. Il mean you *can't* read, can you? You can't read or write.'

Chapter 18

The silence endured for a full minute.

Melinda too had blushed. But although she was aware enough to have guessed at last, her sensitivity didn't extend to understanding how appalling that discovery was for Eunice. She was only twenty.

'Why didn't you tell us?' she said as Eunice got up. 'We'd have understood. Lots of people are dyslexic, thousands of people actually. I did some work on a study of it in my last year at school. Miss Parchman, shall I teach you to read? I'm sure I could. It'd be fun. I could begin in the Easter holidays.'

Eunice took the two mugs and set them on the draining board. She stood still with her back to Melinda. She poured the remains of her tea down the sink. Then she turned round slowly and, with no outward sign that her heart was drumming fast and heavily, fixed Melinda with her apparently emotionless, implacable stare.

'If you tell anyone I'm what you said, that word, I'll tell your dad you've been going with that boy and you're going to have a baby.'

She spoke so levelly and calmly that at first Melinda hardly understood. She had led a sheltered life and no one had ever really threatened her before.

'What did you say?'

'You heard. You tell them and I'll tell them about you.' Abuse wasn't Eunice's forte but she managed. 'Dirty little tart, that's what you are. Dirty interfering little bitch.'

Melinda went white. She got up and walked out of the kitchen, stumbling over her long skirt. Out in the hall her legs almost gave way she was shaking so much, and she sat down in the chair by the grandfather clock. She sat there with her fists pressed to her cheeks till the clock chimed six and the kitchen door opened. A wave of sickness hit her at the thought of even seeing Eunice Parchman again, and she fled into the drawing room where she fell on to the sofa and burst into tears.

It was there that George found her a few minutes later.

'My darling, what is it? What on earth's happened? You mustn't cry like this.' He lifted her and hugged her in his arms. There had been a quarrel, he thought, with that boy, and that was why she had come home to an empty comfortless house. 'Tell Daddy.' He forgot she was twenty. 'Tell me all about it and you'll feel better.'

Jacqueline said nothing but 'I'll leave you two alone'. George never interfered between her and Giles, and she never interposed her voice between him and his children.

'No, Jackie, you're not to go.' Melinda sat up and scrubbed at her eyes. 'Oh, I am a *fool*! I'll tell you both, but it's so awful.'

'As long as you're not ill or hurt,' said George, 'it isn't awful.'

'Oh God.' Melinda swallowed, took a deep breath. 'I'm so glad you've come back!'

'Melinda, please tell us what's the matter.'

'I thought I was going to have a baby but I'm not,' said Melinda in a rush. 'I've been sleeping with Jon since November. I know you'll be cross, I know you'll be disappointed, but I do love him and he loves me and it's all right, really it is, and I'm not going to have a baby.'

'Is that all?' said George.

His daughter stared at him. 'Aren't you mad with me? Aren't you shocked?'

'I'm not even surprised, Melinda. For heaven's sake, d'you think me that much of a fuddy-duddy? D'you think I haven't noticed that things have changed since I was young? I won't say I don't regret it, I won't say I wouldn't rather you hadn't, and I shouldn't like you to be promiscuous. But I'm not in the least shocked.'

'You are *sweet*.' She threw her arms round his neck.

'And now perhaps you'll tell us,' said George disengaging himself, 'why you were crying? I presume you're not sorry you aren't pregnant?'

Melinda managed a watery smile. 'It was that woman – Miss Parchman. It's unbelievable, Daddy but it's true. She found out. She must have overheard me talking on the phone to Jon at Christmas, and when I – well, found out something about her, she said she'd tell you. She threatened me. Just now. She said she'd tell you I was pregnant.'

'*She did what?*'

'I said it was unbelievable.'

'Melinda, of course I believe you. The woman actually blackmailed you?'

'If that's blackmail, yes.'

'What were her exact words?'

Melinda told him. 'And she called me a tart. It was awful.'

Silent until now, Jacqueline spoke. 'She must leave of course. Now. At once.'

'Darling, I'm afraid she must. I know what it means to you, having her, but...'

'It doesn't mean a thing. I never heard anything so odious and revolting in my life. To dare to threaten Melinda! She must be told at once. You'll have to do it, George, I couldn't trust myself.'

He gave her a glance that was passionate in his appreciation of her loyalty. And then, 'What did you find out about her, Melinda?'

Fatal question. It was a pity George hadn't waited to ask it until after he had dismissed Eunice. For his daughter's answer moved him as the substance of that answer had never moved her, and he was softened by pity.

Eunice believed that her threat had succeeded, and a pride in her achievement went a long way towards conquering distress. That great tomboy had looked really upset. She wouldn't give Eunice away, for, as Joan had said, her father would turn her out of the house. The television on for a variety show, she had watched for a quarter of an hour, knitting away, when there came a knock on her door. Melinda. They always came to you after the first shock was over to beg you not to tell. And even though you promised they kept wanting reassurance. It had been that way with the married woman and Annie Cole. Eunice opened the door.

George walked in. 'You can guess why I've come, Miss Parchman. My daughter naturally told me what passed between you. I'm sorry, but I cannot have a person who threatens a member of my family in my household, so you will, of course, leave as soon as possible.'

It was a tremendous shock to Eunice, who said nothing. The programme had been interrupted for the commercials, and the one currently showing consisted mainly of printed words, a list of East Anglian stores. George said, 'We'll have that off, if you don't mind. It can hardly be of interest to *you*.'

Eunice understood. He knew. She who was without sensitivity in all other respects had an acute delicate awareness in this one. And he, watching her, understood too. Her flush and the distortion of her face told him he had gone too far under gross provocation. He had committed that most uncouth of sins, mocked the hunchback's hump.

'You haven't a contract,' he said quickly, 'so I could ask you to leave at once, but all things considered, we'll say a week. That will give you opportunity to look round for other employment. But in the meantime you will please keep to this

153

room and leave the housework to my wife and Mrs Baalham. I am prepared to give you a reference as to your efficiency, but I could give no assurance of your personal integrity.' He went out and closed the door.

It would be hard to imagine Eunice Parchman in tears, and she didn't cry now. Alone in a place where she might have indulged her feelings, she gave no sign of having any. She neither shook nor sighed nor was sick. She turned on the television and watched it, though slumped a little more heavily than usual in her armchair.

Her illiteracy had been known to three people, but to none of them had it come as a sudden and shocking revelation. Her parents had never thought it important. Gradually Mrs Samson had come to know it and to accept it as she accepted that another child in Rainbow Street was a mongol, but it wasn't the kind of thing you talked about, certainly not to Eunice herself. No one had ever talked to her about it; no whole group of people had ever, all at once, become aware of it. In the days that followed, when she was more or less confined to her room, she thought not at all about where she should go or what she should do, what employment she could find or where she could live. She took very little thought for the morrow, for Mrs Samson or Annie Cole would take her in if she turned up on their doorsteps with her cases, but she thought exhaustively about the Coverdales' discovery which she believed must now be spread all over Greeving. It stopped her going out. It stopped her from going to the village store, and once, when Jacqueline was out and Joan called, she didn't respond to Joan's screeched greeting but stayed in hiding upstairs.

It seemed to her that the Coverdales must spend all their time discussing her disability and laughing about it with their friends. She was partly wrong and partly right, for George and Jacqueline were prevented from doing the latter by honourable feelings and also because it would have made them look very foolish not to have realized before that their housekeeper couldn't read. They told people they had dismissed her for insolence. But to each other they did talk quite a lot about it, and even laughed in a wondering way, and longed for next Monday, shutting themselves up in the drawing room when Eunice crept down for her meals.

Unmoved by any feelings of loyalty or duty to her friend, Eunice thought the best thing would be to avoid Joan and escape from Greeving without ever seeing her again. Things were bad enough without Joan's sympathy and solicitude and tedious questions, for by now Joan also must know. Joan, in fact did know. Or, that is, she knew of Eunice's dismissal for the Mrs Higgs, who was distinguished by *not* riding a bike, had told her about it on Tuesday. She waited for Eunice to come, she did her best to get into Lowfield Hall, and when she couldn't she took the only course open to her – even Joan was afraid to telephone – and sent a message.

That year St Valentine's Day fell on a Sunday, so Valentines needs must arrive on the Saturday. None came for the Coverdales, but one did arrive at Lowfield Hall among the birthday cards for George. It was addressed to Eunice, and Jacqueline handed it to her with a quiet 'This is for you, Miss Parchman'.

Both women flushed, both knew Eunice couldn't read it. She took it upstairs and looked in bewilderment at the gaudy picture of two cherubs twining a garland of pink roses around a blue heart. There were bits of writing all over it. Eunice threw it away.

George became fifty-eight on 13 February, and cards came for him from his wife and all his children. *All my love, darling, your Jackie. Many happy returns and love, Paula, Brian, Patrick and little Giles. Love from Audry and Peter. Lots of love, Melinda – see you Saturday afternoon.* Even Giles had sent a card, inappropriately (or very appropriately) a reproduction of Masaccio's *Expulsion from Paradise*. He didn't go so far as to provide a present, though George got a watch to replace his twenty-five-year-old one from Jacqueline, and a record token and book token from his married son and daughter respectively. That night they were going to dine *en famille* at the Angel at Cattingham.

George drove to Stantwich and picked Melinda up at the station. She presented him with a rather awful scarf that looked as if it had come from the Oxfam shop, though it hadn't, and George thanked her lavishly.

'Time I forgot all this nonsense at my advanced age,' he said, 'but none of you will let me.'

'Well,' said Melinda, who had actually been giving a little time to studying one of her set plays, 'who's born the day that I forget to send to Antony shall die a beggar.'

'My God, the child's been doing some work for a change!'

As they entered the house she looked enquiringly at her father, and George understood. 'Upstairs,' he said with a jerk of his head.

Melinda smiled. 'Have you put her under house arrest?'

'In a way. She goes on Monday morning.'

They dressed up to go out, Jacqueline in the cream velvet, Melinda in her spangled blue, and they were an impressive sight as they walked into the hotel dining room. A handsome family, even Giles, who was at any rate tall and thin, not looking at all bad in his one suit and with his spots rather quiescent at the moment.

Afterwards the waiters and the other diners were to wish they had taken more notice of this happy family, this doomed family. They wished they had known, and then they would have listened to the Coverdales' light-hearted conversation, and paid more attention to Jacqueline's appearance, the evidences of Giles's superlative intellect, Melinda's charm, George's distinguished presence. They didn't know, so they had to confess ignorance when the newspaper reporters questioned them or – and this happened more often – invent all kinds of prognostications and doleful premonitions which they were convinced they had been aware of at the time. The police also questioned some of them, and their ignorance was proved by none of them recalling a discussion between the Coverdales that would have been of relevance in solving the case sooner than it was solved.

This conversation was on the subject of a television programme to take place on the following night, a film of a Glyndebourne production of *Don Giovanni,* due to last from seven until after ten.

'Do you have to get back tomorrow night, Melinda?' asked George. 'It seems a pity for you to miss this, it's supposed to be the television event of the year. I could drive you to Stantwich first thing on Monday.'

'I haven't got a lecture on Monday. Nothing till a tutorial at two.'

'What he really means, Melinda,' said her stepmother, laughing, 'is that he wants some moral support in the car when he drives the Parchman to the station.'

'Not at all. I shall have Giles.'

Jacqueline and Melinda laughed. Giles looked up seriously from his duck and green peas. Something moved him. His conversion? The fact that it was George's birthday? Whatever it was, he was inspired for once to say the perfect thing.

'I will never desert Mr Micawber.'

'Thank you, Giles,' said George quietly. There was an odd little silence in which, without speaking or glancing at each other, Giles and his stepfather approached a closeness never before attained. Given time, they might have become friends. No time was to be given them. George cleared his throat and said, 'Seriously, Melinda, why not stay for the film?'

It wasn't the prospect of missing work which made Melinda hesitate, but of missing Jonathan. They had been together every day and almost every night for weeks now. She would miss him painfully tonight. Must she now contemplate another night without him? It seemed selfish to refuse. She loved her father. How wonderful he and Jacqueline had been last week over that hateful business, how loyal and unwavering! And not a word of reproach for her, not even a warning to be careful. But Jonathan...

She had come to a parting of the ways. Ahead of her the road forked. One path led to life and happiness, marriage, children, the other was a dead end, a cul-de-sac. No Through Road. She hesitated. She chose.

'I'll stay,' she said.

From the village store Joan Smith watched the Mercedes pass through the village on its way to the Angel. Five minutes later she was at the Hall, inside the Hall, for she had skipped in her new, thoroughly insane, way through the gun room to surprise Eunice as she sat devouring egg and chips and lemon cheesecake at the kitchen table.

'Oh, Eun, you must be broken-hearted. The base ingratitude after what you've done for them. And for a little thing like that!'

Eunice was not pleased to see her. The 'little thing' must surely be her inability to read. Her appetite gone, she glowered and waited for the worst. Eventually it was not the worst but the best that came, but she had to wait for that.

'All packed, are you, dear? No doubt, you've got plans of your own. Anyone with your skills won't have far to look for a brilliant situation, but I want you to know you're welcome to make your home with us. While Joanie has a spare bed and a roof over her head, you're welcome. Though the Lord only knows how long it'll be spared to us while the wicked man rageth.' Joan panted from her efforts said breathlessly yet coyly, 'Did you get anything by the post today?'

Hard colour came into Eunice's cheeks. 'Why?'

'Oh, she's blushing! Did you think you'd got an admirer in the village, Eun? Well, you have, dear. Me. Why ever didn't you read my message on the back? I knew they'd be out; I said I'd pop up.'

Eunice had supposed Melinda had sent the mocking Valentine. But this wasn't the source of her overwhelming tremendous relief. Joan didn't know, it hadn't reached Joan. Relief threw her back, quite wan and weak, in her chair. She approached love for Joan in that moment, and she couldn't have done enough for her. Recovered and almost ebullient, she made tea, cudgelled her poor imagination to invent details of her dismissal to satisfy Joan, denounced the Coverdales with bitterness, promised Joan her attendance on the following night, her last night, at the temple in Nunchester.

'Our last time together, Eun. And I was counting on your company when Elder Barnstaple and Mrs come to us for supper on Wednesday. But God isn't mocked, dear. You'll rise again in all your glory when he's in the pit, when they're reaping the punishment of their iniquity – oh, yes, when they're heaped with retribution.'

Taking very little notice of all this, of Joan's ravings and prancings, Eunice nevertheless ministered to her like the Martha she was, pouring tea and slicing cheesecake and promising no end of things, like coming back to see Joan at her first opportunity, and writing to her (of all things!) and swearing, in very un-Eunice-like fashion, undying friendship.

Joan seemed to have an instinct about when it was safe to remain and when to go, but this time, so vehement were they and with so much to talk about, that the van had only just turned out of the drive when the Mercedes came up it. Eunice tramped off to bed.

'Back to the grind on Monday,' said Jacqueline, leaving a satiny stripe in the dust where she had run her finger across the surface of her dressing table. 'I feel as if I've had nine months' holiday. Ah, well all good things come to an end.'

'And all bad ones,' said George.

'Don't worry. I'm just as glad as you to see the back of her. Had a nice day, darling?'

'I have had a lovely day. But all my days are lovely with you.'

She got up, smiling at him, and he took her in his arms.

Chapter 19

In church on Sunday morning, their last morning, the Coverdales murmured that they had done those things which they ought not to have done and left undone those things which they ought to have done. They uttered this in a reverent and quite sincere way, but they did not really think about what they were saying. Mr Archer preached a sermon about how one ought to be kind to old people, to one's elderly relatives, which had no bearing on anything in the Coverdales' lives, though plenty on the lives of Eunice Parchman and Joan Smith. After church they had sherry at the Jameson-Kerrs', and lunch was late, not on the table till three.

The weather was non-weather, windless, damp, the sky overcast, but already the first signs of spring had appeared. Early spring is not green but red, as each twig in the hedges takes on a crimson sheen from the rising vitalizing sap. In the garden of Lowfield Hall the snowdrops were coming out, first flowers of spring, the last flowers the Coverdales would ever see.

Melinda had phoned Jonathan before she went to church, speaking to him for the last time. For the last time Giles saw the Elevation of the Mass. Although he was not yet received into the Church, kind Father Madigan had heard his confession and shriven him, and Giles was perhaps in a state of grace. For the last time George and Jacqueline had a Sunday afternoon doze, and at five George moved the television set into the morning room, plugging in the aerial to the socket between the front windows.

When she woke up Jacqueline read the article on *Don Giovanni* in the *Radio Times,* and then she went into the kitchen to make tea. Eunice passed through the kitchen at twenty-five past five in her dark red coat and woolly hat and scarf. The two women pretended not to have seen each other, and Eunice left the house by way of the gun room, closing the door quietly behind her. Melinda fetched her tape recorder, and putting her head round the door of Giles's sanctum, told him she meant to record the opera.

'I suppose you won't even come down for it,' she said.

'I don't know.'

'I wish you would. I'd like you to.'

'All right,' said Giles.

The dark winter's day had slipped, without any apparent sunset, into dark winter's night. There was no wind, no rain, no stars. It was as if the moon had died, for it had not been seen for many nights. All around isolated Lowfield Hall the undulating fields, the deserted threading lanes, and the small crowding woods were enclosed by impenetrable blackness. Not quite impenetrable, for, from the Stantwich road, the traveller would be able to make out the Hall as a brilliant spot of light. How far this little candle throws his beams! So shines a good deed in a naughty world.

Joan and Eunice reached the Epiphany Temple at five to six, and Joan behaved peaceably, perhaps with an ominous quietness, during the hymn-singing and the confessing. Afterwards, while they were eating seed cake and Joan was recounting details of her sinful past to a new member, Mrs Barnstaple came up to her and said rather stiffly that she and the Elder would be unable to visit the Smiths on Wednesday evening. Now the Barnstaples lived in Nunchester, and efficient as the grapevine was, it didn't extend to Nunchester. Mrs Barnstaple had taken her decision because, although she knew Joan was a good Epiphany Person whom the Lord had pardoned, she couldn't (as she told her husband) stomach listening to any more of that stuff about goings-on in Shepherd's Bush while she was eating. But Joan took her refusal as reaction to the news of the inquiry set in train by George Coverdale, and she jumped up, giving a loud scream.

'Woe to the wicked man who spreadeth slanders in the ears of the innocent!' Joan didn't necessarily quote from the Bible. Just as often she ranted in biblical language what she thought ought to have been in the Bible. 'The Lord shall smite him in his loins and in his hip and his thigh. Praised be the Lord who chooseth his handmaid to be his weapon and his right hand!'

Her body was charged with a frenetic energy. She screeched, and spittle sprayed from her mouth. For a few seconds the brethren enjoyed it, but they were not mad, only misguided fanatics, and when Joan's eyes rolled and she began tugging at her hair, actually pulling some of it out, Mrs Barnstaple tried to get hold of her. Joan gave her a great push, and that lady fell backwards into the arms of her husband. Eunice was appealed to, but Eunice didn't want to do anything to antagonize Joan, who was now in control of the whole assembly, raving incomprehensible words and throwing herself backwards and forwards in a frenzy.

Then, as suddenly as she had begun, she stopped. It was mediumistic, the change that came over her. At one moment she seemed possessed by an enraged spirit, the next she had fallen spent and silent into a chair. In a small voice she said to Eunice, 'We'll be on our way when you're ready, Eun.'

They left the temple at twenty past seven, Joan driving like a cautious learner.

Grouped a suitable twenty feet away from the television set, George and Jacqueline sat together on the sofa, Melinda on the floor at her father's feet, Giles hunched in an armchair. The tape recorder was on. Having fidgeted with it during the overture, moving it about and watching it anxiously, Melinda grew less and less aware of its presence as the opera proceeded. She was all set to identify with every female character. She was Ana, she would be Elvira, and, when the time comes, Zerlina too. She leaned her head against George's arm of the sofa, for George, in her eyes, had become the Commendatore, fighting a duel and getting himself killed for his daughter's honour, though she didn't quite see her Jonathan as the Don.

Elegant Jacqueline, in green velvet trousers and gold silk shirt, pencilled a critical note or two on the margin of the *Radio Times.* Under her breath she whispered, following Ottavio, 'Find husband and father in me!' and she darted a soft look at George. But George, being a man, a handsome and sexually successful man, couldn't help identifying with the Don. He didn't want a catalogue of women, he only wanted his Jacqueline and yet...

'I will cut out his heart!' sang Elvira, and they laughed appreciatively, all but Giles. He was only there for Melinda's sake, and the age of reason and manners had never held much appeal for him. He alone heard a footstep on the gravel of the drive at twenty to eight while Scene Two and the Catalogue Song were ending, for he alone was not concentrating on the music. But of course he did nothing about it. That wasn't his way.

Looking indignant, Jacqueline added a line to her notes as Scene Three opened. The time approached five minutes to eight. As Giovanni sang, '*O, guarda, guarda!* Look, look!' the Smiths' van entered the drive of Lowfield Hall and crept, with only sidelights on, almost to the front door. But the Coverdales did not look or hear any extraneous sound. Even Giles heard nothing this time.

Joan's driving had become erratic, and her jerky zigzagging from slow lane to fast was a frightening experience even for phlegmatic Eunice.

164

'You'd better calm down if you don't want us both killed.'

The admonitions of those who seldom remonstrate are more effective than the commands of naggers. But Joan was in no state to adopt the happy mean. It was neck or nothing for her, and she crawled along the lane to Greeving.

'Come in for a bit,' said Eunice.

'That'd be Daniel into the lion's den,' said Joan with a shriek of laughter.

'You come in. Why shouldn't you? A cup of tea'd calm you down.'

'I like your spirit, Eun. Why shouldn't I? They can't kill me, can they?'

Joan kangaroo-hopped the van in too high a gear up the drive. It was Eunice, the non-driver, who grabbed the gear lever and stamped on the clutch so that they could approach more quietly. The van was left standing on the broad gravel space, a little way from the streak of light that fell from between the drawing-room curtains.

'They're looking at the TV,' said Eunice.

She put the kettle on while Joan lingered in the gun room.

'Poor little birds,' she said. 'It doesn't seem right. What have they done to him?'

'What have I done?' said Eunice.

'Too right.' Joan took one of the guns down and levelled it playfully at Eunice. 'Bang, bang, you're dead! Did you ever play cowboys when you were a kid, Eun?'

'I don't know. Come on, tea's ready.' In spite of her defiant words, she was nervous that Joan's hysterical voice would penetrate to the drawing room and be heard above the music. They mounted the first flight of stairs, Eunice carrying the tray, but they never reached the attic floor. Never again was Joan Smith to enter Eunice's domain, and no final farewell was ever to be spoken between them. Jacqueline's bedroom door stood open. Joan went in and put the light on.

Eunice noticed that there was a patina of bedroom dust,

composed of talcum and fluff, on the polished surfaces, and that the bed was less evenly made than when she had made it. She set the tray down on one of the bedside tables and gave the quilt a twitch. Joan tiptoed round the room, lifting her high heels an inch above the carpet and giggling soundlessly on a series of small exhalations like a person imitating a steam engine. When she reached Jacqueline's side of the bed she picked up the photograph of George and laid it face downwards.

'She'll know who did that,' said Eunice.

'Doesn't matter. You said they can't do any more to you.'

'No.' After a small hesitation, Eunice laid the picture of Jacqueline face downwards also. 'Come on, we'd better have that tea.'

Joan said, 'I'll pour.' She lifted the teapot and poured a steady stream into the centre of the counterpane. Eunice retreated, one hand up to her mouth. The liquid lay in a lake, and then it began to seep through the covers.

'You've done it now,' said Eunice.

Joan went out on to the landing and listened. She came back. She picked up a box of talcum, took off the lid and hurled the box on to the bed. White clouds of powder rose, making Eunice cough. And now Joan had opened the wardrobe.

'What are you going to do?' Eunice whispered.

No answer from Joan. She was holding the red silk evening gown on its hanger. She set her fingers in the circle of the neckline and ripped the dress downwards, so that she was holding the front in one hand and the back in the other. Eunice was frightened, she was appalled, but she was also excited. Joan's mounting frenzy had excited her. She too plunged her hands inside the wardrobe where she found the green pleated dress she had so often ironed, and she ran into its bodice the points of Jacqueline's nail scissors. The scissors were snatched from her by Joan who began indiscriminately

166

slashing clothes, gasping with pleasure. Eunice trod heavily on the pile of torn cloth, she ground her heel into the glass of those framed photographs, she pulled out drawers, scattering jewellery and cosmetics and the letters which fluttered from their ribbon binding. It made her laugh throatily while Joan laughed maniacally, and they were both confident that the music from below was loud enough to drown any noise.

It was, for the time being. While Eunice and Joan were making mayhem above their heads, the Coverdales were listening to one of the loudest solos in the whole opera, the Champagne Aria. Jacqueline heard it out, and then she left the drawing room to make coffee, choosing this opportunity because she disliked the Zerlina and feared she would make a hash of *Batti, batti*. In the kitchen she noticed that the kettle was still warm, so Eunice must have come back, and noticed too the shotgun on the table. But she supposed George had put it there for some purpose of his own before they had begun to watch television.

The sound of the drawing-room door opening, and footfalls across the hall floor, sobered Joan and Eunice. They sat down on the bed, looking at each other in a mock-rueful way, eyebrows up, lips caught under upper teeth. Joan switched off the light, and they sat in darkness until they heard Jacqueline cross the hall and re-enter the drawing room.

Eunice kicked at a heap of mingled broken glass and nylon. She said, 'That's torn it,' quite seriously, not joining in Joan's laughter. 'Maybe he'll get the police on us.'

'He doesn't know we're here.' Joan's eyes gleamed. 'Got any wire cutters in the house, Eun?'

'I don't know. Could be in the gun room. What d'you want wire cutters for?'

'You'll see. I'm glad we did it, Eun. O, we have smitten him in his high places, in the bed of his lechery we have afflicted him. I am the instrument of the Lord's vengeance! I am the sword in his hand and the spear in his right hand!'

167

'If you go on like that they'll hear you,' said Eunice. 'I'm glad we did it too.'

They left the tray on the table, the teapot in the middle of the bed. The light was on down in the hall. Joan went straight to the gun room and rooted about in George's tool-box.

'I'm going to cut the phone wire.'

'Like they do on TV,' said Eunice. She had ceased to protest. She nodded approvingly. 'It comes in over the front door,' she said. 'Stop them phoning the police, that will.'

Joan came back, a silent smile glittering. 'What shall we do now, dear?'

It hadn't occurred to Eunice that they would do anything more. Breaking things down here must necessarily be heard in the drawing room, and, police or not, she and this frail stick of a woman could easily be overpowered by four strong adults. 'I don't know,' she said, but this time her habitual response had a wistful note in it. She wanted the fun to go on.

'May as well be hanged for a sheep as a lamb,' said Joan, picking up the shotgun and looking down one of its barrels. 'Frighten them out of their wits, it would, if I fired this.'

Eunice took the other gun off the wall. 'Not like that,' she said. 'Like this.'

'You're a dark horse, Eun. Since when've you been a lady gangster?'

'I've watched him. I can do it as well as he can.'

'I'm going to try!'

'It's not loaded,' said Eunice. 'There's things called cartridges in that drawer. I've often watched him do it. They cost a fortune, those guns, couple of hundred each.'

'We could break them.'

'That's what you call it when you open them to load them. Breaking the gun's what you say.'

They looked at each other and Joan laughed with a sound like a peacock's shriek.

'The music's stopped,' said Eunice.

It was twenty-five minutes to nine. Act One had come to an end, in the opera and in the kitchen.

Chapter 20

In the lull between acts Jacqueline poured second cups of coffee for all of them. Melinda stretched and stood up.

'Marvellous,' said George. 'What do you think, darling?'

'Zerlina's awful. Too old and too tinkly. George, did you hear any sounds from upstairs during the minuet?'

'I don't think so. It was probably our *bête noire* slinking in.'

'The last thing she does is slink, Daddy,' said Melinda. 'Sneaking, maybe. Oh God, I've forgotten to stop the tape.'

'It wasn't slinking or sneaking I heard, but breaking glass.'

Melinda switched off her recorder. 'They were at a party,' she said, referring to the opera. 'I expect it was sound effects.' The rest of what she was going to say was cut off by a thin shriek from somewhere outside the room.

'George!' Jacqueline almost shouted. 'It's that Mrs Smith!'

'I do believe it is,' said George, slowly and ominously.

'She's out in the kitchen with Miss Parchman.'

'Very soon she'll be out in the cold with her marching orders.' He got up.

'Ooh, Daddy, you'll miss the beginning of Act Two. Nasty old Parchment Face is probably just having a farewell party.'

'I'll be two minutes,' said George. He went to the door where he paused and looked at his wife for the last time. Had he known it was the last time, that look would have been eloquent of six years' bliss and of gratitude, but he didn't know, so he merely cast up his eyes and pursed his mouth before walking across the hall and down the passage to the kitchen. Jacqueline considered going with him, but thought better of it and settled back against the sofa cushions as Act Two began with the quarrel between Leporello and his master. The tape recorder was on. *Ma che ho ti fatto, che vuoi lasciarmi?* But what have I done to you that you wish to leave me? *O, niente affato; quasi ammazzarmi!* Oh, nothing at all, but almost killed me...

George opened the kitchen door, and there he stopped in amazement. His housekeeper stood on one side of the table, her stripy hair coming away from its pins, her pale face flushed maroon, facing the crane-chick figure of Joan Smith, befeathered in green and salmon pink. Each was holding one of his shotguns which she pointed at the other.

'This is monstrous,' said George when he recovered his voice. 'Put those guns down at once!'

Joan gave a babbling shriek. 'Bang, bang!' she said. Some memory of war or war film came to her. *Hände hoch!'* she shouted, and pointed the gun at his face.

'Fortunately for you, it isn't loaded.' Calmly Major Coverdale of Alamein looked at his new watch. 'I will give you and Miss Parchman thirty seconds to put those guns on the table. If you don't I shall take them from you by force, and then I shall call the police.'

'You'll be lucky,' said Eunice.

Neither woman moved. George stood stock-still for the full half-minute. He wasn't afraid. The guns weren't loaded. As the thirty seconds came to an end and Joan still pointed the gun at him, he heard faintly from the drawing room the beginning of Elvira's sweet and thrilling *o, taci ingiusto core!* Be silent, treacherous heart! His own was thudding steadily. He went up to Joan, grasped the gun and gave a sharp grunt as Eunice shot him in the neck. He fell across the table, flinging out his arms to grasp its edge, blood shooting in a fountain from the severed jugular. Joan scuttered back against the wall. With an indrawn breath, Eunice fired the second barrel into his back.

At the sound of the two shots Jacqueline sprang to her feet with a cry of alarm. 'For heaven's sake, what was that?'

'Mrs Smith's van backfiring,' said Melinda, and, dropping her voice because of the tape, 'It always does that. There's something wrong with the exhaust.'

'It sounded like a gun.'

'Cars backfiring do sound like guns. Sit down Jackie, or we'll miss this, and it's the loveliest song of all.'

Be silent, treacherous heart. Beat not so in my breast. Elvira leaned from her window, Leporello and the Don appeared beneath it, and the great trio swelled on the two baritone voices and the soprano. Jacqueline sat down, glanced at the door. 'Why doesn't your father come back?' she said nervously.

'He's shot the lunatic,' said Giles, 'and he doesn't know how to tell us.'

'Oh, *Giles.* Darling, go and see, would you? I can't hear a sound.'

'Of course you can't, Jackie, with this on,' said Melinda with asperity. 'You don't *want* to hear him bawling Parchman out, do you? All this rubbish is going to be on my tape, isn't it?'

Jacqueline put up her hands, fluttering them in a little gesture of apology, yet of anxiety too, and Giles who had begun languidly to raise himself from his chair, slumped back into it. From the television came the softly plucked notes of Giovanni's mandoline. *Dei vieni alla finestra.* Then come to the window... Jacqueline, her hands clenched, obeyed his behest. She jumped up suddenly, went to the window on the left of the set and parted the curtains. The tape forgotten, she cried out:

'Mrs Smith's van is out there! It can't have been that we heard.'

She turned back to face them, a disgruntled Melinda, a bored exasperated Giles. Her face was puckered with distress, and even Giles saw it, felt it, her tension and her rising fear.

'I'll go,' he sighed, beginning to shift himself very slowly like an old man with arthritis. He lounged towards the door as Joan Smith and Eunice Parchman passed from the kitchen into the passage.

'We'll have to kill the others now,' said Eunice in the voice she used when speaking of some necessary measure, not to be postponed, such as washing a floor.

Joan, who needed no encouragement, looked back at George. He was dead, but his watch lived on, and since his death the minute hand had passed from the ten nearly to the twelve. It was almost nine o'clock. She looked back once, and then up at Eunice with a great face-splitting smile. There was blood on her hands and face and on the jumper Eunice had knitted for her. They passed into the hall and the strengthening music, music which met them with a blast of baritone voice and plucked strings as Giles opened the drawing-room door. He saw the blood and shouted out.

He shouted, 'Oh Christ!' and turned back, a split second before Joan told him to.

'Get back in there. We've got guns.'

Eunice was the first to follow him. A jumble of male voices singing roared in her head, and power, the chance at last to command and avenge, roared through her body. It strengthened her hands which had failed her a little back there in the kitchen. They were hard and dextrous now as she levelled the reloaded gun. Jacqueline's face, blanched and terrified, was to her only the face which had sneered a little while ago handing over that Valentine. Jacqueline's voice, screaming for her husband, was still the voice of a woman who read books and looked up from her letter-writing to murmur sarcastic courtesies. In those moments the words they cried and their pleas passed over her almost unheard, and by some strange metamorphosis, produced in Eunice's brain, they ceased to be people and became the printed word. They were those things in the bookcases, those patchy black blocks on white paper, eternally her enemies, hated and desired.

'You'd better sit down,' she said. 'You've got it coming to you.'

Joan's laughter cut across her words. Joan shouted something from the Bible, and then Joan fired her gun. Eunice gasped. Not because she heard the screams or saw the blood, but because Joan might do it first, Joan might beat her to it. She advanced, pointing her gun. She fired both barrels, reloaded while another shot rang in her ears, and then she emptied the two barrels into what lay on the Chinese carpet.

The music had stopped. Joan must have stopped it. The banging had stopped and the screaming. A silence more profound, more soothing to the mind and the savage breast, filled the drawing room like a thick tangible balm. It held Eunice suspended. It petrified this stone-age woman into stone. Her eyelids dropped and she breathed evenly and steadily so that, had she had an observer, he would have supposed her fallen asleep where she stood.

A stone that breathed was Eunice, as she had always been.

Chapter 21

The exalted calm of one who has performed a holy mission descended upon Joan Smith. She surveyed what she had done and saw that it was good. She had scattered the enemies of God, and thus purified herself. If the M'Naghten Rules had been applied to her she would have passed the test, for though she had known what she was doing she did not know it was wrong.

She was innocent in the true meaning of the word. And now she would drive down into Greeving and tell the village what she had done, proclaim it in the streets and shout it aloud in the Blue Boar. It was a pity she had cut the phone wire, for otherwise she could have lifted the phone and announced it to the operator. Calmly, majestically, she laid down the gun and picked up the tape recorder. It was still on. She pressed something and the little red light on it went out. Inside it was a record of her achievement, and it is a measure of Joan's madness that at that moment she saw herself, at some future time, playing the tape for the edification of the Epiphany brethren.

Of Eunice she took very little notice. Eunice stood immobile, still holding her gun, staring implacably at the bodies of Giles and Melinda, who lay side by side in death, closer to an embrace than they had ever been in life. But Joan had forgotten who Eunice was. She had forgotten her own name, and the past, and Shepherd's Bush and Norman. She was alone, a titaness, an angel, and she feared nothing but that some malignant spirit, allied to the Coverdale interest, might yet intervene to prevent her from proclaiming the good news.

George's blood was on her jumper, on her hands and face. She let it dry there. Uncharacteristically, with a long slow stride, she walked towards the door and the hall, and Eunice was aroused from her contemplation.

'You'd better wash your face before you go,' she said.

Joan ignored her. She opened the front door and looked for demons in the darkness. The drive and the garden were empty, and to Joan they seemed friendly. She got into the van.

'Suit yourself,' said Eunice. 'Have a good wash before you go to bed. And mind you don't say a word. Just keep quiet.'

'I am the spear of the Lord of Hosts.'

Eunice shrugged. That sort of thing didn't much matter. Joan always went on like that, and the village people would only think she was more crazy than ever. She went back into the house where she had things to see to.

With only sidelights on, Joan drove the van euphorically out of the grounds of Lowfield Hall. She drove with her head held high, looking to the right and the left, anywhere but ahead of her, and she smiled graciously as if to an admiring throng. It was a miracle she even reached the gates. But she did reach them and got about a quarter of a mile along the lane. There, where the lane bent rather sharply to avoid a high brick wall that enclosed the front garden of Mr Meadows' farmhouse, she saw a white owl drop from one of the trees and flap heavily in front of her at windscreen level. Joan thought it was a demon sent by the Coverdales to get her. She stamped on the accelerator to smash through it and smashed instead into the wall. The front part of the van crumpled up like a concertina, and Joan's head crashed through glass into a twelve-inch thick bastion of concrete faced with brick.

It was half past nine. Mr and Mrs Meadows were visiting their married daughter in Gosbury, and there was no one else in the house to hear the crash. Norman Smith was in the Blue Boar where they had had their own bit of excitement, although it wasn't until the following day that they realized how exciting it had been. He went home at ten-fifteen. His van wasn't parked between the village store and the triangle of grass, but he supposed Joan was still off somewhere with Eunice, it being Eunice's last night in Greeving, and a good thing too. No one came down Greeving Lane (or, at least, no one reported the crash) until the Meadowses got home at twenty-five past ten. When they saw their ruined wall and the van with Joan lying unconscious half in and half out of it, they phoned first for an ambulance and then they phoned Norman Smith. Joan, who was alive, though in a bad way, was taken to hospital where they weren't going to worry about whether the blood on her was all hers or not, there was so much of it. So Joan Smith, who ought to have gone into a mental hospital months before, ended up in an intensive-care ward for the physically injured.

This was the second time that evening Norman had been afforded the sight of blood. Very nearly three hours before he was fetched to the scene of his wife's accident, two young men had walked into the saloon bar of the Blue Boar, and the smaller and younger of them had asked the licensee, Edwin Carter, the way to the men's room. He wanted to wash his hands, for the left one appeared injured in some way, and blood had seeped through the handkerchief that bandaged it.

Mr Carter directed him to the lavatory, and his wife asked if there was anything she could do in the way of first aid. Her offer was refused, no explanation of the injury was given, and when the young man came back he had rebandaged his hand with a cleaner handkerchief. Neither of the Carters nor any of the patrons of the bar recalled actually having seen his hand, but only that there had been blood on the original bandage. The other witnesses were Jim Meadows of the garage, Alan and Pat Newstead, Geoff and Barbara Baalham and Geoff's brother Philip, and Norman Smith.

Mrs Carter was to remember that the man with the injured

hand drank a double brandy and his companion a half of bitter. They sat at a table, drank their drinks in less than five minutes, and left without speaking to anyone except to ask where they could get petrol at this hour, Meadows' garage being closed. Geoff Baalham told them there was a self-service petrol station on the main road past Gallows Corner, and, describing how to find it, followed them out on to the Blue Boar's forecourt. There he noticed their car, an old Morris Minor Traveller, maroon bodywork in a wooden shooting brake frame. He didn't, however, notice the registration number.

They left the village by Greeving Lane, their route inevitably taking them past Lowfield Hall.

On the following day all those witnesses furnished the police with descriptions of these strangers. Jim Meadows said they both had long dark hair, were both dressed in blue denim and the one whose hand was not injured was over six feet tall. The Carters agreed that the tall one had long dark hair, but their daughter, Barbara Baalham, said both had brown hair and brown eyes. According to Alan Newstead, the one with the injured hand had short fair hair and piercing blue eyes, but his wife said that, though piercing, the eyes were brown. Geoff Baalham said the short one had fair hair and grey corduroy jeans, while his brother insisted both wore denim jeans and the tall one had bitten nails. Norman Smith said the fair one had a scratch on his face and the dark one was no more than five feet nine.

All of them wished they had taken more notice at the time, but how were they to know they would need to?

Left alone, Eunice, who had wanted to 'see to things', at first saw to nothing at all. She sat on the stairs. She had a curious feeling that if she did nothing but just went off in the morning with her cases to the bus stop she had long ago located and got to London, it would all be all right. They might not find the Coverdales for weeks, and when they did they wouldn't know where she was, would they?

A cup of tea would be nice, for she had never had that earlier one, Joan having poured the contents of the pot all over Jacqueline's bed. She made the tea, walking back and forth past George's body. The watch on his dead wrist told her it was twenty to ten. Now to pack. She had added very little to her personal property during those nine months apart from what were truly consumer goods, sweets, chocolate, cake, and these she had consumed. Only a few hand-knitted garments swelled her stock of clothes. Everything was packed into Mrs Samson's cases in much the same order as it had originally gone in.

Up here, in her room, it felt as if nothing had happened. Pity she had to go tomorrow really, for now there was no one to make her go, and she liked it here, she had always liked it. And it would be even better now that there was no one to interfere with her life.

It was rather early to go to bed, and she didn't think she would be able to sleep. This was exceptional for Eunice who knew she could always sleep as soon as her head touched the pillow. On the other hand, the circumstances were exceptional too, never had she done anything like this before, and she understood this. She understood that all the excitement was bound to keep her awake, so she sat looking round the room, looking at her cases, not feeling in the mood for television and rather wishing she hadn't packed her knitting at the bottom of the big case.

She was still sitting there at a quarter to eleven wondering what time the bus went in the morning and hoping it wouldn't be raining, when she heard the wail of a siren in Greeving Lane. The siren was on the ambulance that had come to fetch Joan Smith, but Eunice didn't know this. She thought it must be the police, and suddenly, for the first time, she was alarmed. She went down to the first floor and Jacqueline's bedroom to see what was going on. She looked out of the window, but she could see nothing and the wailing had died away. As she dropped the curtain, the siren started up again, and after a few moments some vehicle she couldn't see but for its light howled up towards the Hall, passed the Hall, and charged off towards the main road.

Eunice didn't like it. It was very unusual in Greeving. What were they doing? Why were they out there? Her television viewing had taught her a little about police procedure. She put a bed light on and walked about the room, absently wiping every solid article Joan had touched, the broken glass and the ornaments and the teapot. Steve, in her serial when he wasn't shooting people or chasing them in cars, was a great one for fingerprints. The police would be here in a minute, though she could no longer hear their siren. She went downstairs. She went into the drawing room and again put a light on. Now she could see she had been silly, thinking the police wouldn't find out. If they didn't come now, they would come tomorrow, for Geoff Baalham would bring the eggs in the morning, and if he couldn't get in he would look through the window and see George's body. To stop them suspecting her, there were quite a lot of things she must do. Wipe Joan's prints off the wire cutters, for one thing, wipe clean the guns.

She looked around the drawing room. On the sofa, splashed with blood, was an open copy of the *Radio Times*, and along with the bloodstains was some writing. Eunice hated that, far more than the stains. The first thing she should have done was destroy that copy of the *Radio Times,* burnt it in the sink with matches, or cut it up and buried it, or pushed it scrap by scrap down the waste-disposal unit. But she couldn't read. She closed it and, in an attempt to make things look tidier, put it with the Sunday papers in the stack on the coffee table. It bothered her to leave those dirty cups there, but she felt it would be a mistake to wash them up. Putting the television back in its proper place in the morning room would also add to tidiness, and she lugged it across the hall, at last aware that she was quite tired.

There didn't seem anything else to be done, and the police car hadn't come back. Now, for the first time since she had wreaked this havoc, she looked long and steadily at George's body and then, re-entering the drawing room, at the bodies of his wife, his daughter and his stepson. No pity stirred her and no regret. She did not think of love, joy, peace, rest, hope, life, dust, ashes, waste, want, ruin, madness and death, that she had murdered love and blighted life, ruined hope, wasted intellectual potential, ended joy, for she hardly knew what these things are. She did not see that she had left carrion men groaning for burial. She thought it a pity about that good carpet getting in such a mess, and she was glad none of the blood had splashed on to her.

Having spent so much time making things look all right, she was anxious that her good work should be seen. It had always brought her gratification, that the fruit of her labours was admired, though not by a smile or a word had she ever shown her pleasure. Why wait for the police to discover it when she herself was far away? They were about, she thought in her unclear way, they would come quite quickly. The best thing would be for her to tell them without delay. She picked up the phone and had started dialling before she remembered Joan had cut the wires. Never mind, a walk in the fresh air would wake her up.

Eunice Parchman put on her red coat and her woolly hat and scarf. She took a torch from the gun room and set off to walk to Greeving and the phone box outside the village store.

Chapter 22

Detective Chief Superintendent William Vetch arrived in Greeving from Scotland Yard on Monday afternoon to take charge of the Coverdale Massacre Case, the St Valentine's Day Massacre.

He came to a village of which few people in the great world had ever heard, but whose name was now on every front page, blazed from every television screen. He found a village where on this first day the inhabitants remained indoors, as if afraid of the open air, as if that open air had changed its quality overnight and become savage, inimical and threatening. There were people in the village street, but those people were policemen. There were cars, police cars; all night and all day the drive to Lowfield Hall was jammed with the cars and vans of policemen and police photographers and forensic experts. But the people of Greeving were not to be seen, and on that day, 15 February, only five men went to work and only seven children to school.

Vetch took over the village hall, and there he set up a 'murder room'. There, with his officers, he interrogated witnesses, examined evidence, received and made phone calls, spoke to the press – and had his first interview with Eunice Parchman.

He was an experienced officer. He had been a policeman for twenty-six years, and his career in the Murder Squad had been remarkable for displays of courage. He had personally arrested James Timson, the Manchester Bank Killer, and had led the group of officers who charged into the Brixton flat of

Walter Eksteen, an armed man wanted for the murder of two security guards.

Among his juniors he had the reputation of fastening on to one particular witness in each case he handled, of relying on that person for support, and even, according to those who did not like him, of befriending him or her. In the Eksteen case this had paid off, and he had been led to the killer by Eksteen's ex-mistress whose trust he had won. The witness he chose for this role in the Coverdale case was Eunice Parchman.

No one had ever really liked Eunice. In their way her parents had loved her, but that is a different thing. Mrs Samson had pitied her, Annie Cole had feared her, Joan Smith had used her. Bill Vetch actually liked her. From the time of that first interview, he liked her. For Eunice didn't waste words or seem to prevaricate or show misplaced sentimentality, and she wasn't afraid to say when she didn't know.

He respected her for the way in which, having found four dead bodies in circumstances which had sickened the hearts of the police officers who first came, she had walked a mile in the dark to reach a call box. Suspicion of her hardly touched him, and a faint doubt, present before he saw her, vanished when she told him frankly that she had not liked the Coverdales and had been dismissed for insolence. This, anyway, was no middle-aged woman's crime, nor could it have been committed single-handed. And already, before he saw Eunice, he had begun to mount the hunt for the man with the injured hand and his companion.

This is the statement which Eunice had made to the Suffolk officers on the previous night: 'I went to Nunchester with my friend, Mrs Joan Smith, at half past five. We attended a religious service at the Epiphany Temple on North Hill. Mrs Smith drove me back to Lowfield Hall and I got there at five to eight. I looked at the clock in the hall as I came in by the front door and it said five to eight. Mrs Smith did not come in. She had not been feeling well and I told her to go straight home. There was a light on in the hall and in the drawing room. You could see the drawing-room light from outside. The drawing-room door was shut. I did not go into the drawing room. I never did after I had been out in the evening unless Mr or Mrs Coverdale called me. I did not go into the kitchen either as I had had my tea in Nunchester after the service. I went upstairs to my room. Mr and Mrs Coverdale's bedroom door was open but I did not look inside. I did some knitting and then I packed my cases.

'Mr and Mrs Coverdale usually went to bed at about eleven on a Sunday. Giles spent most evenings in his own room. I did not know if he was in his room as the door was shut when I went upstairs. I did not think much about it. I was thinking about leaving on the next day, and I did not go out of my bedroom again until about eleven-thirty.

'It was not necessary for me to go downstairs to wash as I had my own bathroom. I went to bed at eleven. The lights were always left on on the first-floor landing and on the stairs to the second floor. Mr or Mrs Coverdale turned them off when they came to bed. When I could see under my door that the lights were still on at eleven-thirty I got up and went to turn them off. I put on my dressing gown as I had to go down to the first floor to turn that light off. Then I saw some clothes on the floor in Mr and Mrs Coverdale's bedroom, and some broken glass. I had not seen this when I came up because then I had my back to the door. What I saw alarmed me and I went down to the drawing room. There I found the bodies of Mrs Coverdale and Melinda Coverdale and Giles Mont. I found Mr Coverdale dead in the kitchen. I tried to phone the police but could not get the dialling tone, and then I saw that the wire had been cut.

'I heard no unusual sounds between the time I came in and the time I found them. No one was leaving the Hall when I arrived. On my way home I may have passed cars, but I did not notice.'

To this statement Eunice adhered, changing it not in a single particular. Sitting opposite Vetch, her eyes meeting his calmly, she insisted that she had arrived home at five to eight. The grandfather clock had stopped because George had not been there to wind it at ten on Sunday night. Did that clock keep good time? Eunice said it was sometimes slow, she had known it as much as ten minutes slow, and this was confirmed by Eva Baalham and later by Peter Coverdale. But in the days that followed Vetch was often to wish that George's watch had been broken by shot, for of all elements in a murder case he most disliked confusion over time, and the difficulty of fitting the facts to the times was to cause him much frustration.

According to the medical experts, the Coverdales and Giles Mont had met their deaths after seven-thirty and before nine-thirty, rigor mortis having already begun when the bodies were first examined at a quarter past midnight. Its onset is accelerated by heat, and the drawing room and kitchen had been very warm, for the central heating remained on all night at Lowfield Hall in the depths of winter. Many other factors were taken into consideration: stomach contents, post-mortem lividity, changes in cerebro-spinal fluid, but Vetch could not persuade his experts to admit the possibility of death having occurred before half past seven. Not when that heat, a temperature of nearly eighty, was borne in mind, not in the face of Eunice's evidence that the meal the Coverdales had eaten at six – tea and sandwiches and cake – had been completely digested. And Vetch himself thought it odd that a family who had eaten at six should start drinking coffee at, say, seven.

Nevertheless, it could just be made to work out. The two youths in denim had come into the Blue Boar at ten to eight. That gave them fifteen minutes in which to kill the Coverdales – for what motive? For kicks? For some revenge against the social class the Coverdales represented? – and five minutes in which to leave the Hall and drive to Greeving. By the time Eunice came in at five to (or five past) eight, they were a mile away, leaving death and silence behind them.

In that fifteen minutes they must also have ravaged the bedroom, though why they should have poured tea on the bed, Vetch couldn't imagine. Wanton damage, he thought, for none of Jacqueline's jewellery had been taken. Or had they been looking for money, and been surprised in their hasty plundering by one of the Coverdales? At some stage the man with the wounded hand must have removed one of the gloves he was wearing, for gloves had been worn as there were no prints, unless a glove had still been on the hand when shot grazed it. Fifteen minutes was enough, just enough in which to smash and tear and kill.

Vetch spent many hours questioning those patrons of the Blue Boar, among them Norman Smith, who had seen and had spoken to the two young men in denim. And by Monday evening every police force in the country was searching for that car and its occupants.

Joan Smith lay in a coma in Stantwich General Hospital. But Vetch believed she had never entered the Hall that evening, and with her he concerned himself only to check that Eunice had been correct in stating that the two of them had left the Epiphany Temple at seven-twenty. The brethren confirmed it, but not one of them told Vetch's officers that Joan Smith had threatened George Coverdale's life shortly before her departure. They hadn't known it was George she was raving about, and if they had, the conduct and desires of the Epiphany People must be kept from policemen who were not of the elect.

Eunice was allowed to remain at the Hall, for she had nowhere else to go and Vetch wanted her on the spot. The kitchen was open to her but the drawing room was sealed up, and that copy of the *Radio Times* sealed up inside it.

'I don't know,' she said when Vetch asked her if George

Coverdale had had enemies. 'They had a lot of friends. I never heard of anyone threatening Mr Coverdale.' And she made him a cup of tea. While she told him about the Coverdales' life, their friendships, their habits, their tastes, their whims, the murderess and the investigating officer drank their tea at the table, well scrubbed by Eunice, on which George had fallen in death.

What had happened at Lowfield Hall struck the inhabitants of Greeving with incredulity, with horror, and some of them with sick sorrow. Necessarily, nothing else was talked about. Conversations that began on practical matters – what should they have for dinner, how was someone's flu, rain again and bitterly cold, isn't it? – turned inevitably to this massacre, this outrage. Who would do a thing like that? You still can't believe it, can you? Makes you wonder what the world's coming to. Jessica Royston wept and would not be comforted. Mary Cairne had Eleigh's the builders to put up bars at her downstairs windows. The Jameson-Kerrs thought how they would never again go to Lowfield Hall, and the brigadier shuddered when he remembered pheasant shoots with George. Geoff Baalham, mourning Melinda, knew that it would be a long time before he could again bring himself to drive past Gallows Corner on a Friday or Saturday afternoon.

Peter Coverdale and Paula Caswall came to Greeving, and Paula, who was to stay with the Archers, collapsed from shock and grief within hours of her arrival. Peter stayed at the Angel in Cattingham. There, in the cold damp evenings, over the electric fire that inadequately heated his room, he sat drinking with Jeffrey Mont who was staying at the Bull at Marleigh. He didn't like Jeffrey, whom he had never met before and who got through a bottle of whisky a night, but he thought he would have gone mad without someone to talk to, and Jeffrey said that, without his company, he'd have killed himself. They went to the Archers together to see Paula, but Dr Crutchley had put her under sedation.

Jonathan Dexter, in Norwich, first learned of Melinda's death when he read of it in the paper. He did nothing. He did not check or get in touch with his parents or try to get in touch with Peter Coverdale. He shut himself up in his room and remained there, living on stale bread and milkless tea for five days.

Norman Smith went dutifully to visit his wife every evening. He didn't want to go. More or less unconsciously, he would have liked Joan to die because it was very pleasant on his own, but he would no more have said this to himself than he would have avoided going to see her. That was what a husband did when his wife was ill so he did it. But because Joan couldn't move or speak or hear anything, he couldn't tell her the news. Instead he gossiped about it with other visiting husbands, and thrashed it over incessantly in the Blue Boar where he was now able to spend as much time as he liked.

Nothing had been heard from Stantwich as to an inquiry into Joan's interference with the mail. Norman, who still retained some shreds of optimism in spite of what he had been through, supposed this was because the principal witness was dead. Or the postmaster had heard of Joan's accident and didn't like to harass him while his wife was ill.

His van had been towed to a garage in Nunchester. Norman went to Nunchester on the bus to find out about it and was told by the garage proprietor that it was a total write-off. A deal was done for the usable parts of the van, and the garage man said, 'By the way, this was under the back seat,' and gave him an object which Norman thought was a transistor radio.

He took it home with him, put it on a shelf with a pile of copies of *Follow My Star,* and forgot about it for some days.

Chapter 23

Identikit pictures of the two wanted men appeared in every national newspaper on Wednesday, 17 February, but Vetch hadn't much faith in them. If a witness cannot remember whether a man's hair is fair or brown it is unlikely he will recall the shape of that man's nose or forehead. The attendant at the self-service petrol station a hundred yards from Gallows Corner remembered the taller dark one of them. But it was a self-service station, the dark youth had served himself, and had come into the glass fronted office only to pay. The attendant had not even seen the other man, could not say that there had been another man, and remembered the car only because maroon is a fairly unusual colour for a Morris Minor Traveller.

It was from his recollection and that of Jim Meadows, Geoff Baalham and the other Sunday night patrons of the Blue Boar that the pictures had been made up. They evoked hundreds of phone calls to the Murder Room in Greeving Village Hall from people offering sightings of grey or green or black Minor Travellers, or from those who possessed maroon coloured ones respectably locked up in garages. But each one of these calls had to be checked before they could be dismissed.

Appeals were made to every hotel keeper and landlady in the country as to whether any of their guests or tenants possessed a car answering to the description given by Geoff Baalham and the garage attendant. Had it been missing from its usual parking place on Sunday? Where was it now? These appeals resulted in hundreds more phone calls and hundreds of fruitless interviews that continued through Wednesday and Thursday.

But on Thursday a woman who was neither a landlady nor a hotel keeper phoned Vetch and gave him some information about a car answering the description of the wanted vehicle. She lived on a caravan site near Clacton on the coast of Essex, some forty miles from Greeving, and Vetch was talking to her in her own caravan not much more than an hour later.

Residents' cars were parked in a muddy and unsightly section of field adjacent to the entrance of the site, and Mrs Burchall, though possessing no car of her own, had often noticed there a maroon-coloured Traveller because it was the dirtiest vehicle in the park and, because of a flat rear tyre, had sunk lopsidedly into the mud. This car had been in its usual place on the previous Friday, but she couldn't remember whether she had noticed it since. However, it was not there now.

The owner of the car turned out to be, or have been, a man called Dick Scales. Scales, a long-distance lorry driver, wasn't at home when they called at the caravan where he lived, and Vetch and his men talked to a middle-aged Italian woman who called herself Mrs Scales but subsequently admitted she was not married. Vetch could get little out of her beyond cries of *'Mama mia!'* and expostulations that she knew nothing about any car and it was all Dick's fault. She rocked about on a broken chair while she talked, clutching in her arms a fierce-looking little mongrel terrier. When would Dick be back? She didn't know. Tomorrow, next day. And the car? They were not to ask her about cars, she knew nothing of cars, couldn't drive. She had been in Milan with her parents since before Christmas, had only returned last week, and wished now she had never come back to this cold, horrible, godless country.

Police waited for Dick Scales on the M1. Somehow or other they missed him, while Vetch in Clacton wondered uneasily about the set-up. If Scales were guilty, how could the Carters, the Baalhams, the Meadowses and the petrol-station attendant have mistaken a man of fifty for a tall dark youth?

At Lowfield Hall the drawing room remained sealed up, and several times a day, as Eunice came downstairs to the kitchen, she walked past that sealed door. She never thought of trying to get inside the room, although, had she wanted to, it would not have been very difficult. The French windows were locked, but the keys to them hung on their hook in the gun room. To such small oversights as these the police are sometimes prone. But in this respect their lack of caution neither damaged their case nor benefited Eunice, for she had no idea that the one piece of evidence which could incriminate her lay behind that door, and they had already dismissed that evidence, or what they had seen of it, as so much waste paper.

The one piece? Yes, for if she had secured it, been able to read what was written on it, it would have led her by now to that other. More precisely, she would have known what that other was, and when the time came would not have rejected it with unthinking indifference.

She was calm, and she felt herself secure. She watched television and she plundered the deepfreeze to make herself large satisfying meals. Between meals she ate chocolate, more than her usual quota, for though unconscious of any real nervous tension, she found it a little disconcerting to encounter policemen daily. To maintain her stock of supplies, she walked down to the village store where Norman Smith presided alone, chewing gum from force of habit.

That morning he had had a phone call from Mrs Elder Barnstaple to say that she would drop in and collect such copies of *Follow My Star* as Joan had not had time to distribute. Norman took them down from the shelf, and with them the object that had been found in the back of his van. But he didn't show it to Eunice. He mentioned it while selling her three Mars bars.

'Joan didn't borrow a radio from you, did she?'

'I haven't got a radio,' said Eunice, refusing the gift of her future and her liberty. She walked out of the shop without asking after Joan or sending her love. Mildly interested to note that there were fewer police about than usual, she observed the absence of Vetch's car from its usual place outside the village hall. Mrs Barnstaple, just arriving, put hers there instead, and Eunice favoured her with a nod and one of her tight smiles.

Norman Smith took his second visitor into the parlour.

'That's a nice little tape recorder you've got there,' said Mrs Barnstaple.

'Is that what it is? I thought it was a radio.'

Again Mrs Barnstaple averred it was a tape recorder, and said that if it wasn't Norman's, to whom did it belong? Norman said he didn't know, it had been found in the van after Joan's accident, and perhaps it belonged to one of the Epiphany brethren. In Mrs Barnstaple's view, this was unlikely, but she would make enquiries.

Almost anyone with a spark of curiosity in his make-up would, after the object's function had been defined, have fiddled about with it and made it play. Not Norman. He was pretty sure he'd only get hymns or confessions out of it, so he put it back on the now empty shelf and went back to sell Barbara Baalham an air letter.

Some hours before, as a worried Dick Scales was beginning the drive from Hendon in north-west London to his home in Clacton, a young man with long dark hair walked into Hendon Police Station and, in a manner of speaking, gave himself up.

Friday, the day of the funeral.

It took place at two in the afternoon, and it was well attended. The press came along with a few carefully chosen policemen. Brian Caswall came from London and Audrey

Coverdale from the Potteries. Jeffrey Mont, the worse (or perhaps the better) for drink, was there, and so were Eunice Parchman, the Jameson-Kerrs, the Roystons, Mary Cairne, Baalhams, Meadowses, Higgses and Newsteads. Under a blue sky, as brilliant as on the day Giles Caswall was christened, the closest mourners followed the Rector from the church door along a little winding path to the south-east corner of the churchyard. Rugged elms and yew trees' shade, and an east wind blowing; George Coverdale had bought a plot under those yews, and in this grave his body and the bodies of his wife and daughter were laid to rest.

Mr Archer spoke these words from the Wisdom of Solomon: 'For though they be punished in the sight of men, yet is their hope full of immortality. And having being a little chastized, they shall be greatly rewarded...'

Giles, at his father's request, was cremated at Stantwich, and there were no flowers at the brief service that was held for him. The wreaths that came for the Coverdales never reached the destination for which Peter intended them, Stantwich Hospital – to decorate Joan Smith's bedside? – but shrivelled within an hour in the February frost. At the suggestion of Eva Baalham, Eunice sent a sheaf of chrysanthemums, but she never paid the bill the florist sent her a week later.

She was driven back to the Hall by Peter who advised her to go upstairs and lie down, a suggestion which met with no opposition from Eunice, thinking of her television and her Mars bars. In her absence and that of the police, in the terrible silence and the harsh cold, he took away the kitchen table, chopped it to pieces and burnt it down by the blackthorn hedge while the frosty crimson sun went down.

Vetch did not attend the funeral. He was in London. There he heard from Keith Lovat the story which had been told to the Hendon police, and accompanied by Lovat, he went to the house in West Hendon where Michael Scales rented one furnished room and Lovat another. At the end of the garden were three lock-up garages, surrounded by a high fence. On the concrete behind this fence and at the side of the garages, Vetch was shown what appeared to be a car concealed by a canvas cover. Lovat removed the cover to disclose a maroon-coloured Morris Minor Traveller which he told Vetch he had bought from Michael's father, Dick Scales, on the previous Sunday.

The car, Lovat said, had been for sale for eighty pounds, and he and Michael had gone up to Clacton by train to take a look at it. They arrived there at three and had a meal in the caravan with Dick Scales and the Italian woman whom Lovat called Maria and referred to as Michael's stepmother.

'Maria had this little dog,' Lovat went on. 'She'd brought it back with her from Italy in a basket with a cover over it, and she'd got it through Customs without them knowing. It was a snappy little devil, and I left it alone, but Mike kept playing with it, teasing it really.' He looked at Vetch. 'That was how it all happened, that was the cause of it.'

The flat tyre on the car having been changed for the spare one, he and Michael Scales decided to leave for home in it at seven, but not to take the A12 from Nunchester, a fast road which would have taken them in to East London. Instead they intended to go westwards to Gosbury and then south for Dunmow and Ongar, entering London by the A11 and the North Circular road to Hendon. But before they left Michael was again playing with the dog, offering it a piece of chocolate and snatching it away when the dog came to take it. The result of this was that the dog bit him on his left hand.

'We went just the same. Maria tied Mike's hand up with a handkerchief, and I said he'd better have it seen to when we got home. Dick and Maria got into a bit of a panic on account of her bringing the dog in like that, and Dick said they could get fined hundreds and hundreds if they got caught. Well, Mike promised he wouldn't go to a doctor or a hospital or anything, though the blood was coming through the bandage by then. We started off, and the fact is I lost my way. The lanes were pitch-dark, and I thought I'd missed the Gosbury road, though it turned out I was really on it. Mike didn't know anything about people not being allowed to bring animals into the country without putting them in quarantine, so I told him a bit about that, and when he said why not, I said it was on account of not spreading rabies. That really scared him, that was the beginning of it.'

They had turned into what was evidently Greeving Lane. The time? About twenty to eight, Lovat said. At the Blue Boar in Greeving Michael washed his hand and had a double brandy. They were directed to a self-service petrol station on the Gosbury Road which, Lovat realized, was the road they had mistakenly left half an hour before.

'Mike had got into a state by then. He was scared he'd get rabies and didn't want to go to the hospital in case he got his dad into trouble. We got home around eleven, I couldn't get more than forty out of the car, and when we got home I parked it down there and put that cover over it.'

Lowfield Hall? said Vetch. They must have passed Lowfield Hall twice on their way into and out of Greeving.

For the first time Lovat's voice faltered. He hadn't noticed a single house while driving along Greeving Lane. Strange, thought Vetch, when you remembered that Meadows' farmhouse on its raised ground loomed over the only real bend in the road. But for the time being he let it pass, and Lovat went on to say that on the Tuesday he had realized it was he and Michael Scales for whom the police were hunting. He begged Michael to go with him to their local police station, but Michael, who had been in touch with Dick Scales by phone, refused. His hand had begun to fester and swell, and he hadn't been to work since Wednesday.

On Thursday morning Dick Scales phoned the Hendon house from a call box in the north of England, and when he heard of his son's state he said he would call in on his way south. He reached Hendon at nine in the evening, and he and Michael and Keith Lovat had sat up all night, discussing what they should do. Dick wanted Michael to go to a doctor and say he had been bitten by a stray dog, mentioning nothing about the car or his visit to the caravan, and Michael was in favour of this. Lovat had been unable to make them see his point of view, that all the time they were getting themselves deeper into trouble, and could be charged with obstructing the police. Moreover, he was prevented from having repairs done to the car and, as far as he could see, from using it perhaps for months. At last he decided to act on his own. When Dick had gone he walked out of the house and went to Hendon Police Station.

It was a story not entirely consistent with this one that Vetch finally elicited from Michael Scales. Scales was lying in bed in a filthy room, his arm swollen up to the elbow and streaked with long red lines, and at the appearance of Vetch and his sergeant he began to sob. When Vetch told him that he knew all about the car, the possibly rabid dog and the visit to the Blue Boar at Greeving, he admitted everything – and admitted something about which Lovat had evidently stalled. On their way into Greeving they had stopped at the entrance to the drive of a large well-lighted house, and Lovat had gone up the drive to ask for directions to Gosbury. However, before he reached the door his courage had failed him, on account, Scales said, of the clothes he was wearing and the dirt he had got on himself from tinkering with the car.

After some prevarication, Lovat admitted this. 'I never knocked on the door,' he said. 'I didn't want to scare the people, not at night-time and in a lonely place like that.'

It could be true. Lovat and Scales struck Vetch as being as pusillanimous and indecisive a pair as he had ever come across. Describe the house, he said, and Lovat said it was a big place with two long windows on either side of the front door, adding that he had heard *music coming from the house* as he hesitated on the drive. The time? Twenty to eight, said Lovat, and Scales said nearer a quarter to.

Vetch had Maria Scales charged with contravening the quarantine laws, and Michael Scales was removed to hospital where he was put into isolation. What to do with Lovat? There was as yet insufficient evidence to charge them with the murder, but by some string-pulling Vetch arranged with the resident medical officer to have Lovat taken into hospital also and kept in under observation. There, they were out of harm's way for the present, and Vetch, with a breathing space, considered what he had been told about the time and the music.

What music? The Coverdales' record player, radio and television set were all in the morning room. Therefore it looked as if the music had been an invention of Lovat's, though there seemed no reason why he should have invented it. More probably he and Scales had arrived much earlier at Lowfield Hall, and had killed the Coverdales – for what reason? It wasn't up to Vetch to find a reason. But they could have entered the Hall to wash, to cadge a drink, to use a phone, and had perhaps met with physical opposition from George Coverdale and his stepson. It fitted, and the time, if Lovat were lying, also fitted. But Lovat had to be sure of one thing to start with, or as he told himself in the days that followed, face the music.

It was to the young Coverdales that he went for help, and at once Audrey Coverdale told him what had been perplexing her and yet what had seemed irrelevant to the discovery of the perpetrators of the crime.

'I've never been able to understand why they weren't watching *Don Giovanni*. Jacqueline wouldn't have missed that for the world. It's like saying an ardent football fan would miss the Cup Final.'

But the television set was in the morning room, and they couldn't have been in the morning room from seven onwards, for they had taken coffee in the drawing room, and no amount of juggling with time could make that coffee-drinking take place before seven. On the other hand, guilty or not, Lovat had said he had heard music. On Sunday afternoon Vetch broke the seals on the drawing-room door and revisited the scene of the crime. He was looking for signs that the television set had been in this room, but finding none, it occurred to him to check on the time the opera had begun. Vetch could easily have secured himself a copy of the *Radio Times* for that week from any newsagent. He still does not know to this day what made him pick up the *Observer* from the coffee table on the chance a *Radio Times* might have been underneath it. But it was. He opened it at the relevant page and noticed that page was splashed with blood. If anyone had previously observed this, he had not been told of it. In the margin, between and beneath the blood splashes, were three scribbled notes:

Overture cut. Surely no ascending seventh in last bar of La Ci Darem. *Check with M's recording.*

Vetch had seen enough examples of Jacqueline's handwriting to recognize that these notes had been made by her. And clearly they had been made by her while watching this particular broadcast. Therefore she had watched it or part of it. And, beyond a doubt, it had begun at seven. The only expert he had immediately to hand – and how much of an expert she was he couldn't tell as he knew nothing of music – was Audrey Coverdale. He had the door resealed and lingered for ten minutes to drink the tea Eunice Parchman had made for him. While he chatted with her and Eunice told him she had heard no music when she came in at five to (or five past) eight, that the television set was always in the morning room and had been in the morning room at the time of her discovery of the bodies, the *Radio Times* was a few feet from her, shut up in his briefcase.

Audrey Coverdale was preparing to leave, for she had to be back at work in the morning. She confirmed that the notes were in Jacqueline's hand and quailed at the bloodstains, glad that her husband was not present to see them.

'What does it mean?' said Vetch.

'*La Ci Darem* is a duet in the third scene of the first act.' Audrey could have sung every aria from *Don Giovanni* and told Vetch, within minutes, the precise time at which each would occur. 'If you want to know when it comes, it'd be – let me see – about forty minutes after the beginning.'

Twenty to eight. Vetch simply didn't believe her. It was useless consulting amateurs. On Monday morning he sent his sergeant into Stantwich to buy a complete recording of the opera. It was played on a borrowed player in the Murder Room in the village hall, and to Vetch's astonishment and dismay, *La Ci Darem* occurred almost exactly where Audrey had said it would, forty-two minutes after the commencement of the overture. *Overture cut*, Jacqueline had written. Perhaps the whole opera had been cut. Vetch got on to the BBC who let him have their own recording. The opera had been slightly cut, but only by three minutes in the first three scenes of the first act, and *La Ci Darem* occurred in the recording at seven thirty-nine. Therefore, Jacqueline Coverdale had been alive at seven thirty-nine, had been tranquil, at ease, concentrating on a television programme. It was impossibly far-fetched to suppose that her killers had even entered the house by that time. Yet Lovat and Scales had been seen in the Blue Boar at ten to eight by nine independent witnesses. Someone else had entered Lowfield Hall after Lovat's departure and before five past – it now had to be five *past* – eight.

Vetch studied Jacqueline's notes, almost the only piece of concrete evidence he had.

Chapter 24

Looking through the Wanted column in the *East Anglian Daily Times,* Norman Smith found an insertion from a man who was seeking a second-hand tape recorder. He didn't hesitate for long before picking up the phone. Mrs Barnstaple's enquiries had not found the tape recorder's owner, Joan still lay speechless, unable in any way to communicate, but it didn't cross Norman's mind to take the thing to the police. Or, rather, it crossed his mind only to be dismissed as too trivial when the police were obviously occupied with matters of more moment. Besides, he might get fifty pounds for it, and this would be most welcome in his present penurious car-less state. Fifty pounds, added to the miserable sum for which the van had been insured, would just about buy him a replacement of much the same vintage as the wrecked green one. He dialled the number. The advertiser was a freelance journalist called John Plover who told Norman he would drive over to Greeving on the following day.

Which he did. Not only did he buy the tape recorder on the spot, but he also gave Norman a lift into Stantwich in time for the hospital visiting hour.

In the meantime, Vetch was extracting more information from the notes in the margin of the *Radio Times. Check with M's recording* didn't seem of much significance. He had already checked with two recordings – though not in pursuit of a spurious ascending seventh, whatever that might be – and nothing could shift that aria or put it ten minutes before the time it had actually occurred. Unless Jacqueline had made the note *before* she heard the aria on television, had been listening during the afternoon to a record of Melinda's, and wanted to check with the televised opera. But what she had written was the very reverse of that. Moreover, he was unable to find any record of *Don Giovanni* or any part of it in Lowfield Hall.

'I don't think my sister had any records of classical music,' said Peter Coverdale, and then, 'but my father gave her a tape recorder for Christmas.'

Vetch stared at him. For the first time he realized that a recording need not necessarily mean a black disc. 'There's no tape recorder in the house.'

'I expect she took it back to university with her.'

The possibility which this opened to Vetch was beyond any realistic policeman's dreams – that Melinda Coverdale had actually been recording when the killers came into the house, that the time might thus be precisely fixed, and the intruders' voices preserved. He refused to allow himself to speculate about that aspect of it. The first thing the killers would have done was remove the tapes and destroy them, then rid themselves of the recorder itself. The invaluable Eunice, the star witness, was called in.

She said, 'I remember her dad giving it to her at Christmas. It was in her room in a leather case, and I used to dust it. She took it to college when she went back in January and she never brought it home after that.' Eunice was speaking the truth. She hadn't seen the tape recorder since the morning she had listened in to Melinda's phone conversation. Joan had carried it out from the Hall, Joan who in her madness was a thousand times more sophisticated than Eunice would ever be, and Eunice had not even noticed she had anything in her hand.

While Vetch's men were scouring Galwich for that tape recorder, interrogating everyone Melinda had known, Eunice marched the two miles to Gallows Corner and caught the bus for Stantwich. In a side room off the Blanche Tomlin ward she found Norman Smith sitting by his wife's bedside. She hadn't bothered to tell him she was coming. She had come for the same reason that he came, because it was the thing to do. Just as you went to the weddings and the funerals of people you knew, so you went to the hospital to see them when they were ill. Joan was very ill. She lay on her back with her eyes closed, and but for the rise and fall of the bedclothes, you would have thought she was dead. Eunice looked at her face. She was interested to see what that stretched canvas looked like without paint on it. Stretched canvas was what it looked like, yellow-brown, striated. She didn't speak to it.

'Keep it nice, don't they?' she said to Norman after she had made sure there was no dust under the bed. Perhaps he thought she was speaking of his wife who was also 'kept nice', anchored to her drip-feed, tucked up under a clean sheet, for he made no reply. They were both hoping, for different reasons, that Joan would go on like that for ever, and going home together on the bus, each expressed the pious wish that such a vegetable existence would not be prolonged.

In forlorn hope, Vetch ordered a search of Lowfield Hall, including the long-disused cellar, and when that brought nothing to light, they began digging up the frost-bound flowerbeds.

Eunice didn't know what they were looking for, and she was very little concerned. She made cups of tea and carried it out to them, the policemen's friend. Of much more moment to her were her wages or, rather, the lack of them. George Coverdale had always paid her her month's money on the last Friday in the month. That last Friday, 26 February, would be tomorrow, but so far Peter Coverdale had given no sign that he intended to honour this obligation inherited from his father, which seemed to Eunice very remiss of him. She wasn't going to use the phone. She walked over to Cattingham and enquired for him at the Angel. But Peter was out. Peter, though Eunice didn't know this, was driving his sister back to London to her husband and her children.

Vetch appeared at the Hall on the following morning, and Eunice resolved that he should be her go-between. And this Scotland Yard Chief Superintendent, Vetch of the Murder Squad, was only too happy to oblige. Of course he would get in touch with Peter Coverdale during the day, with pleasure he would apprise him of Miss Parchman's dilemma.

'I've baked a chocolate cake,' said Eunice. 'I'll bring you a bit with your tea, shall I?'

'Most kind of you, Miss Parchman.'

As it happened, it wasn't a bit but the whole cake which Eunice was forced to sacrifice, for Vetch had chosen eleven o'-clock to hold a conference in the morning room with three high-ranking officers of the Suffolk Constabulary. She left him with a quiet 'Thank you, sir', and returned to the kitchen to think about getting her own lunch. And she was eating it at noon sharp, eating it off the counter in the absence of the table, when Vetch's sergeant walked in through the gun room with a young man Eunice had never seen before in tow.

The sergeant was carrying a large brown envelope with something bulky inside it. He gave Eunice a pleasant smile and asked her if Mr Vetch was about.

'In the morning room,' said Eunice, knowing full well whom you sir-ed and whom you didn't. 'He's got a lot of folks with him.'

'Thanks. We'll find our own way.' The sergeant made for the door to the hall, but the young man stopped and stared at Eunice. All the colour had gone out his face. His eyes went wide and he flinched as if she'd sworn at him instead of speaking perfectly normally. He reminded her of Melinda in this same kitchen three weeks back, and she was quite relieved when the sergeant said, 'This way, Mr Plover,' and hustled him out.

Eunice washed the dishes by hand and ate up her last bar of chocolate. Her last bar, indeed. She wondered if Vetch had yet done anything about Peter Coverdale and her wages. Outside they were still digging up the garden, in the east wind, under occasional flurries of snow. Her favourite serial tonight, Lieutenant Steve in Hollywood or maybe Malibu Beach, but she would enjoy it far more if she could be sure her money was forthcoming. She went out into the hall and heard music.

Music was coming from behind the morning-room door. That meant they couldn't be doing anything very important in there, nothing that wouldn't bear a polite interruption The music was familiar; she had heard it before. Sung by her father? On the television? Someone was singing foreign words, so it couldn't have been one of Dad's.

Eunice raised her fist to knock on the door, let it fall again as a voice from within the room shouted above the music:

'Oh Christ!'

She couldn't identify that voice, but she knew the one that came next, a voice silenced now by massive brain injury.

'Get back in there. We've got guns.'

And the others. And her own. All blending with the music vying with it, drowning it in frenzy and fear.

'Where's my husband?'

'He's in the kitchen. He's dead.'

'You're mad, you're crazy! I want my husband, let me go to my husband. Giles, the phone...! No, no... Giles!'

Eunice spoke to Eunice across the days. 'You'd better sit down. You've got it coming to you.'

A cackle from Joan. 'I am the instrument of One Above,' and a shot. Another. Through the music and the screams, the sound of something heavy falling. 'Please, please!' from the girl, and the reloaded guns fired for the last time. Music, music. Silence.

Eunice thought she would go upstairs and repack her things before retribution came from whatever it was in there that acted out, in some way beyond her understanding, the deaths of the Coverdales. But a numbness stunned her mind, and she was less than ever capable of reasoning. She began to walk towards the stairs relying on that strong body that had always done so well by her. And then that body which was all she had, failed her. At the foot of the stairs, on the very spot where she had first stood on entering the Hall nine months before, where wonderingly she had seen herself reflected in a long mirror, her legs gave way and Eunice Parchman fainted.

The sound of her falling reached Vetch who was nerving himself to play the tape once more to an audience of policemen, white-faced now and rigid in their chairs. He came out and found her where she lay, but he could not bring himself to lift her up or even touch her with his hands.

Chapter 25

Joan Smith still lies speechless and immobile in Stantwich General Hospital. She is in a machine which keeps her heart and lungs functioning, and the medical powers that be are at present deciding whether it might not be a mercy to switch that machine off. Her husband is a clerk in a post office in Wales, and he still keeps the name of Smith. There are, after all, a lot of them about.

Peter Coverdale still lectures on political economy in the Potteries. His sister Paula has never recovered from the deaths of her father and Melinda, and she has had three sessions of electro-convulsive therapy in the past two years. Jeffrey Mont is drinking heavily and almost qualifies for the destination in which Joan Smith placed him at her second meeting with Eunice Parchman. These three are engaged in continuous litigation, for it has never been established whether Jacqueline pre-deceased her son or he her. If she died first, Giles briefly inherited Lowfield Hall, and thus it must now be his father's, the property of his next of kin. But if he died before his mother the Hall should pass to George's natural heirs. Bleak House.

Jonathan Dexter, tipped for a first-class Honours degree, got a third. But that was in the early days. He teaches French at a comprehensive school in Essex, has nearly forgotten Melinda, and is going steady with a member of the science department.

Barbara Baalham gave birth to a daughter whom they

called Anne because Melinda, which was Geoff's original choice, seemed a bit morbid. Eva cleans for Mrs Jameson-Kerr and gets seventy-five pence an hour. They still talk about the St Valentine's Day Massacre in Greeving, expecially in the Blue Boar on summer evenings when the tourists come.

Eunice Parchman was tried at the Old Bailey, the Central Criminal Court, because they could not find an unbiased jury for the assizes at Bury St Edmunds. She was sentenced to life imprisonment, but in practice may not serve more than fifteen years. Some said it was an absurdly inadequate punishment. But Eunice was punished. The crushing blow came before verdict or sentence. It came when her counsel told the world, the judge, the prosecution, the policemen, the public gallery, the reporters scribbling away in the press box, that she could not read or write.

'Illiterate?' said Mr Justice Manaton. 'You cannot read?'

She answered when he pressed her. She answered, crimson-faced and shaking, and saw those who were not freaks or disabled as she was write it down.

They have tried to reform Eunice by encouraging her to remedy her basic defect. Steadfastly, she refuses to have anything to do with it. It is too late. Too late to change her or avert what she did and what she caused.

Dust, Ashes, Waste, Want, Ruin, Despair, Madness, Death, Cunning, Folly, Words, Wigs, Rags, Sheepskin, Plunder, Precedent, Jargon, Gammon and Spinach.